Dear Readers,

How to Train Your Dragon is a true story, and it is a story about growing up.

For as I say myself, at the beginning of *How to Steal a Dragon's Sword*:

'… sometimes we do not realise it at the time, but the story we are all a part of is not just a story about Vikings and islands and dragons. It is a story about growing up. And one of the things about growing up, one of the inescapable, inevitable laws, is that one day… One day… One day… It is going to happen. I am sorry, but it's true.'

And look!

It has happened.

Unbelievable, inconceivable.

The first book of *How to Train Your Dragon* was published *twenty years* ago now.

And I drew the very first pictures of Hiccup (who is really me) and his father Stoick the Vast (who is really my own father) twenty-*five* years ago when I had just had a baby, my eldest child, Maisie.

I drew those pictures because there is a moment after you've just had a baby that every parent will recognise, when you think to yourself: 'They're going to let me out of hospital with a *baby*? But I know nothing about babies!'

So you start finding out about babies and looking back to your own childhood, and thinking about how *you* were brought up, and what kind of parent you would ideally want to be.

It could have been *How to Train Your Baby*, really.

This is why every line, every setting, every character, however extraordinary and fantastical and unlikely they may seem, *everything* in *How to Train Your Dragon* has a strange kind of truth to it.

The Isle of Berk is a real place, a wild little island in Scotland. An uninhabited isle so small that when you stand on the top of it you can see sea all around you. An island where I grew up and my children grew up and I first set my foot on that island over *fifty* years ago now.

See how we're going back in time even further!

So the writing in the books is a complicated mixture of memories of my childhood, and the here-and-now of bringing up my own children.

The dragons are sometimes dragons that I created myself on rainy August days back on that Scottish island when I was nine years old. And other times they are dragons that made my son Xanny laugh when he got much

older and enjoyed me reading the books to him. And when Hiccup sets out in his

little boat, *The Hopeful Puffin*, it is sometimes Hiccup, and it is sometimes *me* setting out into those unpredictable Hebridean seas in a rubber dinghy with my siblings, untroubled by adults and with absolutely no life jackets, in the long-ago 1970s, when wild childhoods were a normal part of growing up.

When Hiccup talks to Toothless it is sometimes Hiccup talking, but sometimes it is *me* talking to my own children who grew up over the fifteen-year process of the writing of the books.

It was always my hope for these books to be enjoyed by adult and child together. The books are written to be read aloud, because books read to you live with you all your life. Every book starts and ends with the voice of Hiccup as an old man looking back on his childhood because I am trying to get the person reading aloud to go back to a long-ago lost time when they themselves believed in dragons, and heroes, and witches, just as strongly and innocently as the child sitting listening there beside them.

So when, in honour of the 20th anniversary edition, I am writing a story set in the *How to Train Your Dragon* world for the first time in eight long years, revisiting this place is a deeply haunting, joyous, but bittersweet experience.

For this precious world is a world that has *gone...*

And here is the thing about stories.

The crucible of the story will change those who read it, the characters within it, and the person who is telling it, all at the same time.

I have returned, in the writing of this short story, to a time three-quarters of the way through the *How to Train Your Dragon* story arc, before the Dragon Rebellion happens, and I have tried to recapture the innocence of that time, when Hiccup was still learning to be a dragon trainer, and I was still learning to be a writer and an illustrator, and neither of us yet knew what a Hero Hiccup was going to have to be.

In this new story, I have tried to introduce more of the world-building illustrations that I have learnt how to do on the way of my own journey, and to capture some of the joy and the splendour of flying on the back of a dragon that the movies brought to the world.

And I have finished on a note that is not intended to be a tease, exactly, more of an opening to myself, if I ever wanted to tell stories set in that world in the future.

In the meantime…

Thank you.

Thank you to everyone who has loved *How to Train Your Dragon*, and made it part of their own childhoods, and their own family narratives.

Thank you to the many adults over the past twenty years who have put on wonderful performances of Gobber the Belch and Stoick the Vast, and Toothless, bringing alive the joy of books and the astonishing benefits of reading to the children in their lives. Those children being read to twenty years ago have grown up, too, and are reading and recommending the books to children today. (There is no greater joy, as an author.)

Thank you to my publishers at Hachette, in particular Anne McNeil, Becky Logan, Ruth Alltimes and Naomi Greenwood, and my agents Caroline Walsh and Nicky Lund. Thank you to the incomparable David Tennant for his magnificent readings of the books, and the film-makers, in particular Dean DeBlois, and Chris Sanders and Bonnie Arnold and Chris Kuser, and the incredible music of John Powell – but really to everyone at DreamWorks, who put their hearts and their imaginations into bringing this world to the screen.

And ultimately, I want to say thank you, always and forever, to my own family.

To my father, the giant who brought the dragons into my life, and who died five years ago.

To my husband Simon, my anchor and my star.

And to my three children, Maisie, Clemmie, and Xanny.

That baby in the car seat, Maisie, just turned twenty-five years old. A quarter of a century passed in the blink of an eye.

Clemmie is twenty-two.

And Xan is nineteen.

Here is what I learnt in the writing of these stories.

It wasn't *How to Train Your Baby* after all.

It was *How to Train Your Parent*.

Bringing up children, and writing for children, is just as much about what you learn from *them*, as what you are trying to teach.

Listen to your children.

I have learnt so much from my own children's imagination, their creativity, their positivity, their intelligence and their lack of prejudice.

I am so proud of these three young adults.

And in my head, if I close my eyes, I can still see them playing, still hear them talking, chatting to each other endlessly, never still, never quiet, oh my *goodness* those children were lively. One-year-old Maisie. Two-year-old Clemmie. Three-year-old Xanny.

Growing and changing in time. And yet…

… forever young.

Thank you. Cressida Cowell

20TH

ANNIVERSARY EDITION

HOW TO TRAIN YOUR DRAGON

written and illustrated by

CRESSIDA COWELL

HODDER CHILDREN'S BOOKS

How to Train Your Dragon first published in Great Britain in 2003
How to Train Your Hogfly first published in 2023
This hardback edition published in 2023 by Hodder & Stoughton Limited

1 3 5 7 9 10 8 6 4 2

How to Train Your Dragon
Text and illustrations copyright © Cressida Cowell, 2003

How to Train Your Hogfly
Text and illustrations copyright © Cressida Cowell, 2023

The moral rights of the author has been asserted.

A CIP catalogue record for this book
is available from the British Library.

ISBN 978 1 444 97300 6

Printed and bound in Great Britain by Clays Ltd, Elcograf S.p.A

The paper and board used in this book
are made from wood from responsible sources.

Hodder Children's Books
An imprint of
Hachette Children's Group
Part of Hodder & Stoughton Limited
Carmelite House
50 Victoria Embankment
London EC4Y 0DZ

An Hachette UK Company
www.hachette.co.uk

www.hachettechildrens.co.uk

to my father

JOIN HICCUP ON HIS QUEST

(although he doesn't quite realise he is on one yet...)

THE PROPHECY OF

THE KING'S LOST THINGS

'The Dragontime
is coming
And only a King can save you now.
The King shall be the
Champion of Champions.

You shall know the King
By the King's Lost Things.
A fang-free dragon, my second-best sword,
My Roman shield,
An arrow-from-the-land-that-does-not-exist,
The heart's stone, the key-that-opens-all-locks,
The ticking-thing, the Throne, the Crown.

And last and best of all the ten,
The Dragon Jewel shall save all men.'

Hiccup

Speedifist

Tuffnut Junior

DOGSBREATH THE DUHBRAIN

WARTIHOG

~Novices of the Hairy Hooligan tribe~

clueless

STOICK THE VAST

Fishlegs

Snotlout

GOBBER
THE BELCH

CONTENTS

~ CONTENTS ~

ISLE of BERK
Caliban Caves
Wild Dragon Cliff
Hooligan Village
Madman's Gully
Black Heart Bay
Highest Point
HUGE HILL
Harbour
Hooligan
The Little Isles
Cowrie Beach
Puffin Point

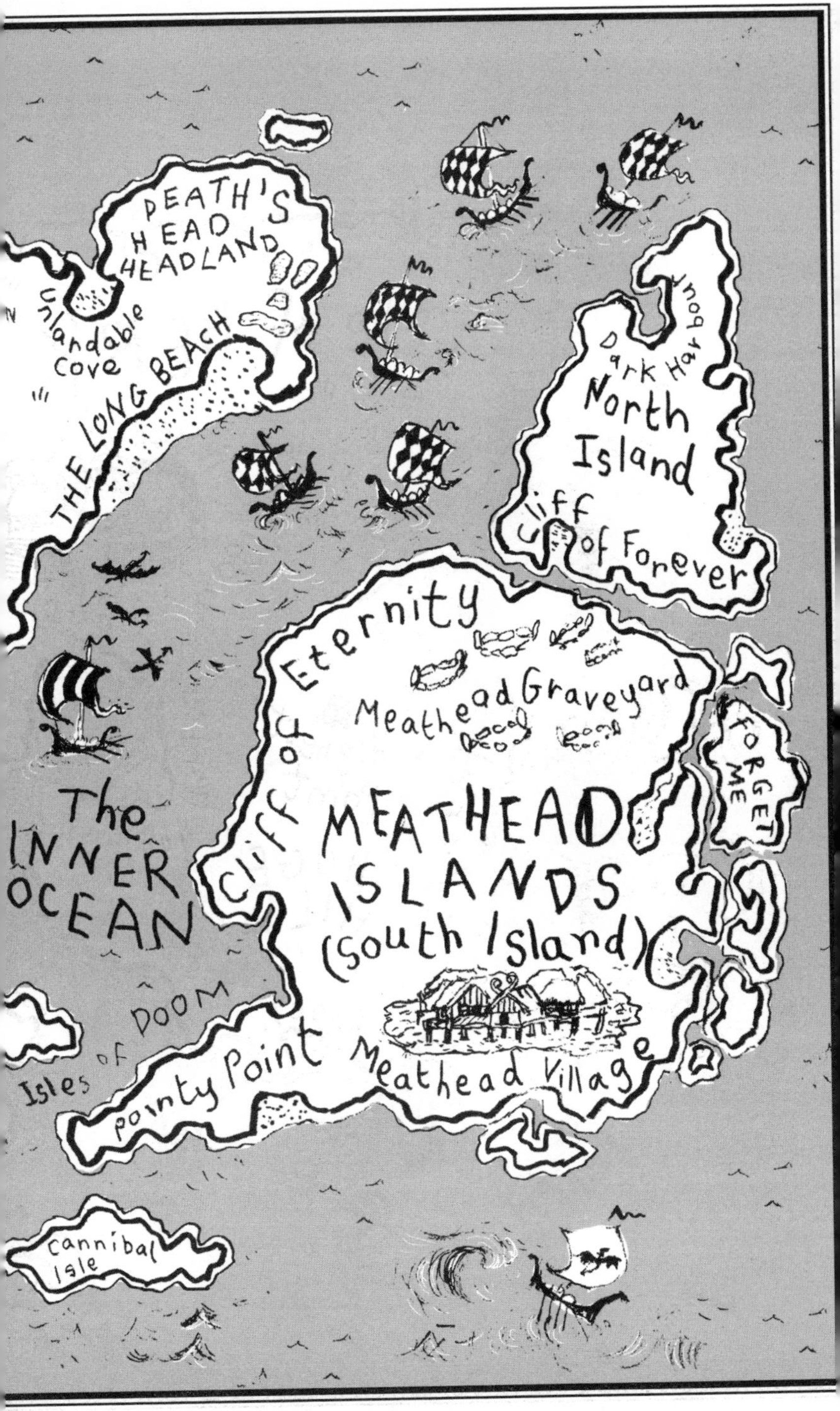
DEATH'S HEAD HEADLAND
Unlandable Cove
THE LONG BEACH
Dark Harbour
North Island
Cliff of Forever
Cliff of Eternity
Meathead Graveyard
FORGET ME
MEATHEAD ISLANDS (South Island)
The INNER OCEAN
Isles of DOOM
pointy Point
Meathead Village
Cannibal Isle

Hiccup
Horrendous
Haddock
the
Third

A Note from Hiccup

There were dragons when I was a boy.

There were great, grim, sky dragons that nested on the cliff tops like gigantic scary birds. Little, brown, scuttly dragons that hunted down the mice and rats in well-organised packs. Preposterously huge Sea Dragons that were twenty times as big as the Big Blue Whale and who killed for the fun of it.

You will have to take my word for it, for the dragons are disappearing so fast they may soon become extinct.

Nobody knows what is happening. They are crawling back into the sea from whence they came, leaving not a bone, not a fang, in the earth for the men of the future to remember them by.

So, in order that these amazing creatures should not be forgotten, I will tell this true story from my childhood.

I was not the sort of boy who could train a dragon with the mere lifting of an eyebrow. I was not a natural at the Heroism business. I had to work at it. This is the story of becoming a Hero the Hard Way.

1. FIRST CATCH YOUR DRAGON

Long ago, on the wild and windy isle of Berk, a smallish Viking with a longish name stood up to his ankles in snow.

Hiccup Horrendous Haddock the Third, the Hope and Heir to the Tribe of the Hairy Hooligans, had been feeling slightly sick ever since he woke up that morning.

Ten boys, including Hiccup, were hoping to become full members of the Tribe by passing the Dragon Initiation Programme. They were standing on a bleak little beach at the bleakest spot on the whole bleak island. A heavy snow was falling.

'PAY ATTENTION!' screamed Gobber the Belch, the soldier in charge of teaching Initiation. 'This will be your first military operation, and Hiccup will be commanding the team.'

'Oh, not Hic-cup,' groaned Dogsbreath the Duhbrain and most of the other boys. 'You can't put Hiccup in charge, sir, he's USELESS.'

Hiccup Horrendous Haddock the Third, the

GOBBER the Belch
Idiot in charge of
Initiation

Hope and Heir to the Tribe of the Hairy
Hooligans, wiped his nose
miserably on his sleeve. He sank a little
deeper into the snow.

'ANYBODY would be better than
Hiccup,' sneered Snotface Snotlout. 'Even
Fishlegs would be better than Hiccup.'

Fishlegs had a squint that made him as
blind as a jellyfish, and an allergy to reptiles.

'SILENCE!' roared Gobber the Belch. 'The
next boy to speak has limpets for lunch for the next
THREE WEEKS!'

There was absolute silence immediately. Limpets
are a bit like worms and a bit like snot and a lot less
tasty than either.

'Hiccup will be in charge and that is an order!'
screamed Gobber, who didn't do noises quieter than
screaming. He was a six-and-a-half-foot giant with a mad
glint in his one working eye and a beard like exploding
fireworks. Despite the freezing cold he was wearing
hairy shorts and a teeny weeny deerskin vest
that showed off his lobster-red skin and
bulging muscles. He was holding a
flaming torch in one gigantic fist.

4

'Hiccup will be leading you, although he is, admittedly, completely useless, because Hiccup is the son of the CHIEF, and that's the way things go with us Vikings. Where do you think you are, the REPUBLIC OF ROME? Anyway, that is the least of your problems today. You are here to prove yourself as a Viking Hero. And it is an ancient tradition of the Hooligan Tribe that you should' – Gobber paused dramatically –

'FIRST CATCH YOUR DRAGON!'

Ohhhhhh suffering scallops, thought Hiccup.

'Our dragons are what set us apart!' bellowed Gobber. 'Lesser humans train hawks to hunt for them, horses to carry them. It is only the VIKING HEROES who dare to tame the wildest, most dangerous creatures on earth.'

Gobber spat solemnly into the snow. 'There are three parts to the Dragon Initiation Test. The first and most dangerous part is a test of your courage and skill at burglary. If you wish to enter the Hairy Hooligan Tribe, you must first catch your dragon. And that is WHY,' continued Gobber, at full volume, 'I have brought you to this scenic spot. Take a look at Wild Dragon Cliff itself.'

The ten boys tipped their heads backwards.

The cliff loomed dizzyingly high above them, black and sinister. In summer you could barely even see the cliff as dragons of all shapes and sizes swarmed over it, snapping and biting and sending up a cacophony of noise that could be heard all over Berk.

But in winter the dragons were hibernating and the cliff fell silent, except for the ominous, low rumble of their snores. Hiccup could feel the vibrations through his sandals.

'Now,' said Gobber, 'do you notice those four caves about halfway up the cliff, grouped roughly in the shape of a skull?'

The boys nodded.

'Inside the cave that would be the right eye of the skull is the Dragon Nursery, where there are, AT THIS VERY MOMENT, three thousand young dragons having their last few weeks of winter sleep.'

'OOOOOOOH,' muttered the boys excitedly.

Hiccup swallowed hard. He happened to know considerably more about dragons than anybody else there. Ever since he was a small boy, he'd been fascinated by the creatures. He'd spent hour after long hour dragon-watching in secret. (Dragon-spotters were thought to be geeks and nerds, hence the need for secrecy.) And what Hiccup had learnt about dragons told him that walking into a cave with three thousand dragons in it was an act of madness.

No one else seemed too concerned, however.

'In a few minutes I want you to take one of these baskets and start climbing the cliff,' commanded Gobber the Belch. 'Once you are at the cave entrance, you are on your own. I am too large to squeeze my way into the tunnels that lead to the Dragon Nursery. You will enter the cave QUIETLY– and that means you too, Wartihog, unless you want to become the first spring meal for three thousand hungry dragons, HA HA HA HA!'

Gobber laughed heartily at his little joke, then continued. 'Dragons this size are normally fairly harmless to man, but in these numbers they will set upon you like piranhas. There'd be nothing left of even a fatso like you, Wartihog – just a pile of bones

DRAGON BASKET

DRAGON goes in HERE

and your helmet. HA HA HA HA! So… you will walk QUIETLY through the cave and each boy will steal ONE sleeping dragon. Lift the dragon GENTLY from the rock and place it in your basket. Any questions so far?'

Nobody had any questions.

'In the unlikely event that you DO wake the dragons – and you would have to be IDIOTICALLY STUPID to do so – run like thunder for the entrance to the cave. Dragons do not like cold weather and the snow will probably stop them in their tracks.'

8

Probably? thought Hiccup. *Oh, well*, that's *reassuring*.

'I suggest that you spend a little time choosing your dragon. It is important to get one the correct size. This will be the dragon that hunts fish for you, and pulls down deer for you. You will catch the dragon that will carry you into battle later on, when you are much older and a Warrior of the Tribe. But, nonetheless, you want an impressive animal, so a rough guide would be, choose the biggest creature that will fit into your basket. Don't linger for TOO long in there—'

Linger??? thought Hiccup. *In a cave full of three thousand sleeping* DRAGONS?

'I need not tell you,' Gobber continued cheerfully, 'that if you return to this spot *without* a dragon, it is hardly worth coming back at all. Anybody who FAILS this task will be put into immediate exile. The Hairy Hooligan Tribe has no use for FAILURES. Only the strong can belong.'

Unhappily, Hiccup looked round at the distant horizon. Nothing but snow and sea as far as the eye could see. Exile didn't look too promising, either.

'RIGHT,' said Gobber briskly. 'Each boy take a

basket to put their dragon in and we'll get going.'

The boys rushed to get their baskets, chattering happily and excitedly.

'I'm going to get one of those Monstrous Nightmare ones with the extra-extendable claws, they're really scary,' boasted Snotlout.

'Oh shut up, Snotlout, you can't,' said Speedifist. 'Only Hiccup can have a Monstrous Nightmare, you have to be the son of a chief.' Hiccup's father was Stoick the Vast, the fearsome chief of the Hairy Hooligan tribe.

'HIC-CUP?!' sneered Snotlout. 'If he's as useless at this as he is at Bashyball, we'll be lucky if he even gets one of the Basic Browns.'

The Basic Brown was the most common type of dragon, a serviceable beast but without much glamour.

'SHUDDUP AND GET INTO LINE YOU MISERABLE TADPOLES!' yelled Gobber the Belch.

The boys scrambled into their places, baskets on their backs, and stood to attention. Gobber walked along the line, lighting the torch that each boy held in front of him from the great flare in his hand.

'IN HALF AN HOUR'S TIME YOU WILL BE A VIKING WARRIOR, WITH YOUR FAITHFUL

THE COMMON OR GARDEN and THE BASIC BROWN

The Common or Garden
or
Basic Brown

The Common or Garden
and the Basic Brown are so
similar that they can be dealt
with together. These are the
most familiar breeds – the ones we
instantly think of when we say 'dragons'.
They are poor hunters, but they are easy
to train. These dragons are the best kind
for family pets, although, as with a lion or
a tiger, they should never be left
unsupervised with very young children.

~ STATISTICS ~

COLOURS: Green and yellow, all shades of brown.
ARMED WITH: Basic teeth and claws.
FEAR FACTOR:.................... **3**
ATTACK:.................... **3**
SPEED:................. **4**
SIZE:....................... **4**
DISOBEDIENCE: **1**

SERPENT AT YOUR SIDE... OR
BREAKFASTING WITH WODEN IN VALHALLA
WITH DRAGON'S TEETH IN YOUR BOTTOM!'
screamed Gobber with horrible enthusiasm.

'DEATH OR GLORY!' yelled Gobber.

'DEATH OR GLORY!' yelled eight boys back at
him fanatically.

Death, thought Hiccup and Fishlegs, sadly.

Gobber paused
dramatically, with the horn
to his lips.

*I think this could
possibly be the worst
moment of my life* SO
FAR, thought Hiccup
to himself, as he waited
for the blast of the horn.
*And if they shout much
louder we're going to wake
up those dragons before we
even* START.

'PARRRRRRRRRP!'
Gobber blew the horn.

2. INSIDE THE DRAGON NURSERY

You have probably guessed by now that Hiccup was not your natural Viking Hero.

For a start, he didn't **LOOK** like a Hero. Somebody like Snotlout, for instance, was tall, muscley, covered in skeleton tattoos, and already had the beginnings of a small moustache. This consisted of a few straggly yellow hairs clinging to his upper lip and was deeply unpleasant to look at, but still impressively manly for a boy not yet thirteen.

Hiccup was on the small side and had the kind of face that was almost entirely unmemorable. He **DID** have Heroic Hair, which was a very bright red and stood up vertically

Snotlout

14

however much you tried to wet it down with sea-water. But nobody ever saw that because it was hidden under his helmet most of the time.

You would NEVER have picked Hiccup out of those ten boys to be the Hero of this story. Snotlout was good at everything and a natural leader. Dogsbreath was as tall as his father and could do amusing things like farting to the tune of the Berk National Anthem.

Hiccup was just absolutely average, the kind of unremarkable, skinny, freckled boy who was easy to overlook in a crowd.

So, when Gobber blew the horn and moved out of sight to find a comfortable rock to sit on and eat his mussel-and-tomato sandwich, Snotlout pushed Hiccup out of the way and took charge.

'OK, listen up, boys,' he whispered in a menacing fashion. 'I'M in charge, not the Useless. And

15

anybody who objects gets a knuckle sandwich from Dogsbreath the Duhbrain.'

'Ugh,' grunted Dogsbreath, pounding his fists together in happy excitement. Dogsbreath was Snotlout's chief sidekick and a great, big gorilla of a boy.

'Bash him, Dogsbreath, to show what I mean...'

Dogsbreath was delighted to oblige. He gave Hiccup a shove that sent him sprawling head first into the snow, then ground his face in it.

'Pay attention!' hissed Snotlout. The boys dragged their eyes away from Dogsbreath and Hiccup and paid attention. 'Rope yourselves together. The best climber should go first...'

'Well, that's YOU of course, Snotlout,' said Fishlegs. 'You're the best at everything, aren't you?'

Snotlout looked at Fishlegs suspiciously. It was difficult to tell whether Fishlegs was laughing at him or not, because of his squint.

'That's right, Fishlegs,' said Snotlout. 'I AM.' And, just in case he *had* been laughing at him: 'Bash him, Dogsbreath!'

While Dogsbreath pushed Fishlegs down to join Hiccup in the snow, Snotlout bossily ordered everybody to rope themselves together.

Hiccup and Fishlegs were the last to be tied on, just behind a flushed and triumphant Dogsbreath.

'Oh brilliant,' muttered Fishlegs. 'I'm about to enter a cave full of man-eating reptiles tied up to eight complete maniacs.'

'If we *get* to the cave...' said Hiccup nervously, looking up at the sheer black cliff.

Hiccup put the lighted torch between his teeth to leave his hands free, and started climbing after the others.

♥ ♥ ♥

It was a perilous climb. The rocks were slippery with snow and the other boys were thoroughly over-excited, making the ascent far too quickly. At one point Clueless missed his footing and fell – luckily on to Dogsbreath, who caught him by the back of the trousers and heaved him back on to the rock again, before he brought the whole lot of them down.

When they finally made it to the mouth of the cave, Hiccup looked down briefly at the sea pounding the rocks way below, and swallowed very hard...

'Untie the ropes!' ordered Snotlout, his eyes popping with excitement at the thought of the dangers to come. 'Hiccup goes into the cave first because HE is the son of the Chief...' He sneered. 'And, if any of the dragons ARE awake, he'll be the first to know about it! Once we're in the cave, it's every man for himself. Only the strong can belong...'

Although he wasn't your usual mindless thug of a Hooligan, Hiccup wasn't a wimp, either. Being frightened is not the same as being a coward. Maybe he *was* as brave as anyone else there, because he went to catch a dragon *despite* knowing what dragons are like. And, when he had climbed perilously to the mouth of the cave and had found that inside there was a long, twisty tunnel, he *still* went down it, despite not being too keen on long, twisty tunnels with dragons at the end of them.

The tunnel was dripping and clammy. At times it was high enough for the boys to walk upright. Then it would close down into narrow, claustrophobic holes that the boys could only just squeeze through, squirming on their stomachs, with the flares held in their mouths.

After ten long minutes of walking and crawling into the heart of the cliff, the stench of dragon – a salty stink of seaweed and old mackerel heads – got stronger and stronger, until finally it became unbearable and the tunnel opened out into a ginormous cavern.

The cavern was full of more dragons than Hiccup could ever have imagined existed.

They were every possible colour and size, and they included all the species that Hiccup had heard of, and quite a few more that he hadn't.

Hiccup started sweating as he looked around him at pile after pile of the animals, draped over every available surface; even hanging upside-down from the roof like giant bats. They were all fast asleep, and most of them were snoring in unison. This was a sound so loud and so deep that it seemed to penetrate right into Hiccup's body and vibrate around his soft insides, churning his stomach and bowels, and forcing his heart to beat at the same slow dragon pulse.

If one, just *one*, of these countless creatures were to wake up, it would raise the alarm to the others and the boys would meet a horrible death. Hiccup had once seen a deer that had wandered too close to Wild Dragon Cliff torn to pieces in a matter of minutes…

Hiccup closed his eyes. 'I will NOT think about it,' he said to himself. 'I WILL NOT.'

None of the other boys were thinking about it.

Ignorance is very useful in such circumstances. Their eyes were popping with excitement as they walked through the cave, hands over their noses to keep out the revolting smell, looking for the biggest dragon they could find that would fit in their basket.

They left the torches in a pile at the entrance. The cavern was already well-lit by the Glowworms, huge, sluggish animals dotted here and there that shone with a steady yet dim fluorescence, like a low-watt lightbulb. And the Flamehuffers gave off extra little bursts of light that flickered on and off as they breathed in and out.

Predictably, most of the boys headed towards the plug-uglies of the dragon world.

Snotlout made a big fuss about grabbing a vicious-looking Monstrous Nightmare, smiling nastily at Hiccup as he did so. Snotlout was the son of Baggybum the Beerbelly, Stoick the Vast's younger brother. He was intending to get rid of Hiccup some time in the future so that he, Snotlout, would become Chief of the Hairy Hooligan Tribe. And a gruesome and terrifying Chief, as Snotlout meant to be, would need a properly awesome dragon.

Wartihog and Dogsbreath got into a loudly whispered fight over a Gronckle, a heavily-armoured brute with fangs like kitchen knives sticking out in such numbers that it couldn't keep its mouth shut. Dogsbreath won, then managed to drop it as he was trying to bundle it into his basket. The weaponry of the beast made a horribly loud clatter as it landed on the floor of the cavern.

The Gronckle opened its evil, crocodile eyes.

Everybody held their breath.

The Gronckle stared ahead. It was difficult to tell from its blank expression whether it was awake or fast asleep. Hiccup realised, in an agony of suspense, that the gossamer-thin third eyelid was still down.

And there it stayed for a few heart-stopping moments, until…

It slowly closed its upper eyelids again.

Amazingly, not one of the other dragons woke up. A few grumbled groggily before making themselves comfy again. But most were in such a stupor that they barely even stirred.

Hiccup let out his breath slowly. Maybe these dragons were so dead to the world that *nothing*

THE GRONCKLE

Extra thick SKULL

a nasty case of dragon ACNE

The Gronckle is the plug-ugly of the dragon world. But what it lacks in looks, it makes up for on the battle-field. They can be slow and, dare I say it, stupid ~ and sometimes they get so fat that they are unable to take off. They are also prone to dragon acne.

~ STATISTICS ~

COLOURS: Snot green, bogey beige, pooey brown.

ARMED WITH: All the best in dragon weaponry. Fangs like daggers, extra spike on neck, ball with spikes on end of tail.

FEAR FACTOR: 7

ATTACK: 8

SPEED: 8

SIZE: 7

DISOBEDIENCE: 5

would wake them.

He swallowed hard, muttered a prayer to Loki, the patron saint of sneaky exploits, and edged forward cautiously to grab the most unconscious-looking dragon, so he could get out of this nightmare as fast as possible.

♦ ♦ ♦

It is a little-known fact that dragons grow colder the deeper they sleep.

It is even possible for a dragon to go into a Sleep Coma in which they are icy-cold, with no obvious pulse, or breath, or heartbeat. They can stay in this state for centuries, and only a highly-skilled expert can tell from looking at them if they are alive or dead.

But a dragon who is awake or lightly sleeping is very warm indeed, like bread that has just come out of the oven.

Hiccup found one that was about the right size and fairly cool to the touch and manoeuvred it into his basket as quickly and carefully as he could. It was a very basic Basic Brown, but at that moment Hiccup could not have cared less. Even though it was barely half-grown, it was surprisingly heavy.

'I DID it, I DID it, I DID it!' he chanted happily to himself. At least he wasn't going to be the only boy in the class who didn't have a dragon. Everybody seemed to have got themselves one by now and they were all making their way quietly towards the exit. Everybody, that was, except for…

… Fishlegs, who was already covered in a bright red, itchy rash, and was at that very moment approaching a pile of knottily entangled Nadders on very loud tiptoes.

Fishlegs was even worse at burglary than Dogsbreath.

Hiccup stopped dead in his tracks. 'Don't do it, Fishlegs – PLEASE don't do it!' he whispered.

But Fishlegs was fed up of Snotlout's taunting and of being sneered at and jeered at. He was going to get himself a really cool dragon that all the other boys would respect.

Squinting so hard he could barely see the pile of dragons, his eyes streaming, and scratching himself violently, Fishlegs reached slowly towards the bottom-most dragon, took one leg in his hand, and gently … yanked.

The entire pile came crashing down in a furious

tangle of limbs and wings and ears. Every boy in the cavern gave a horrified gasp.

Most of the Nadders snapped crossly at each other before settling back down to sleep.

One brute bigger than the others opened his eyes and blinked a few times.

Hiccup noted, with great relief, that the third eyelid was still down.

The boys waited for the eyes to close.

And then Fishlegs sneezed.

Four GIGANTIC sneezes that went echoing and bouncing off the cavern walls.

The big Nadder stared sightlessly ahead, frozen like a dragon statue.

But ve-ry faintly, an ominous purring noise began in his throat.

And ve-ry slowly...

... the third eyelid slid upward.

'Uh-oh,' whispered Hiccup.

The Nadder's head suddenly whipped round to face Fishlegs, its yellow cat's eyes snapping into focus on the boy. It unfolded its wings to their greatest extent and stealthily advanced, like a panther about to spring. It opened its mouth wide enough to show the

25

forked dragon tongue and…

'R-R-R-U-U-U-U-U-N-N-N!' shouted Hiccup, grabbing Fishlegs's arm and dragging him away.

The boys ran for the exit tunnel. Fishlegs and Hiccup were the last to get there.

There was no time to pick up the torches, so they were running in the pitch dark. The basket with the Basic Brown dragon in it was bumping on Hiccup's back.

They had two minutes start on the dragons because it took a while for the first dragon to wake everybody else up. But Hiccup could hear a furious roaring and flapping as the dragons started to pour into the tunnel after the boys.

He ran a little faster.

The dragons could move more quickly than the boys because they could see better in the dark, but they were held up when the tunnel got smaller, because they had to fold their wings up to squirm through.

'I… haven't… got… a… dragon,' panted Fishlegs, a couple of paces behind Hiccup.

'That,' said Hiccup, as he scrambled frantically on his elbows through a narrow bit, 'is the LEAST…

ow… of our problems. They're gaining on us!'

'No… dragon,' repeated Fishlegs stubbornly.

'Oh, for THOR'S SAKE,' snapped Hiccup.

He thrust his basket into Fishlegs's arms and grabbed the empty one from Fishlegs's back. 'Have MINE, then. Wait here.'

And Hiccup turned and went back through the narrow bit even though the roaring was getting louder and closer by the second.

'WHAT… ARE… YOU… DOING???' screamed Fishlegs, frantically dancing up and down on the spot.

Hiccup came back through the hole again precious moments later. Fishlegs grabbed hold of an arm to help haul him through.

The Flight from the Dragon Nursery

They could hear a horrible snuffling as what sounded like the nose of a dragon entered the other end of the hole. Hiccup bunged a rock at it and it squealed indignantly.

They turned a corner and suddenly they could see light from outside at the end of the final tunnel.

Fishlegs went first, but, just as Hiccup was kneeling down to follow, a dragon pounced on him with a flap and a shriek. Hiccup hit it and it fell back enough for him to crawl towards the light. Another dragon – or maybe the same one – sank its fangs into Hiccup's calf. He was so desperate to get out he dragged the animal through with him.

As soon as Hiccup's head and shoulders were through into the light, there was Gobber. He grabbed Hiccup under the armpits and hauled him out, dragons pouring after him.

'JUMP!' yelled Gobber, as he stunned a dragon with one blow of his mighty fist.

'What do you *mean*, JUMP??' Hiccup hesitated as he looked down at the dizzying drop into the sea.

'No time to climb down,' panted Gobber, banging a couple of dragons' heads together, and bouncing three more off his gigantic belly. 'JUMP!!!'

28

Hiccup closed his eyes and leapt off the cliff.

As he plunged through the air, the dragon that was attached to his leg released its jaws with a squawk of alarm and flew off.

Hiccup was travelling at such speed by the time he hit the water that it didn't feel like water at all, more like something hard and painful, and so cold that he nearly passed out.

He spluttered to the surface, amazed to find that he didn't appear to be dead, and was immediately drenched by the gigantic splash of Gobber the Belch landing a couple of feet away from him.

Shrieking furiously, the dragons swarmed out of the cave and dive-bombed the floating Vikings.

Hiccup pulled his helmet as far down as it would go. There were horrible scraping sounds as dragons' talons raked across the metal. Another one landed, hissing, on the water right in front of Hiccup's face. It took off again with a screech when it felt how cold the sea was. The dragons didn't like flying through the snow and, with relief, Hiccup watched as they flew back to scream terrible dragon insults in Dragonese from the warmth of the cave entrance.

Gobber started to pull the boys out of the sea

29

and on to the rocks. Viking boys are strong swimmers but it is difficult to keep afloat when you have a basket full of trapped, terrified dragon on your back. Hiccup was the last to be saved – just in time, as the cold was beginning to put him to sleep.

Well, at least that wasn't DEATH, thought Hiccup, as Gobber grabbed him by the neck to rescue him, nearly drowning him again in the process – but it certainly wasn't GLORY, either.

3. HEROES OR EXILES

The boys scrambled over the slimy pebbles at the edge of the beach and back up Madman's Gully, the gorge they had climbed through a couple of hours before. This was a narrow crack in the cliffs filled with large rocks. They tried to move as quickly as they could, but this is difficult when you are slipping and sliding over huge stones covered in ice, and they made painfully slow progress.

A dragon that *hadn't* been put off by the snow came shrieking down into the gorge. He landed on Wartihog's back and started savaging him, sinking his fangs into Wartihog's shoulder and ripping red lines into his arms. Gobber bashed the dragon on the nose with the handle of his axe, and the dragon let go and flapped away.

But a whole wave of dragons replaced him, pouring into the canyon with awful, rasping cries, fire shooting from their nostrils and melting the snow before them, talons spread wickedly as they swooped downward.

Gobber stood, legs wide apart, and whirled his big, double-headed axe. He threw back his great,

hairy head and yelled a terrible primeval Yell, that
echoed down the sides of the gorge and made the hairs
on the back of Hiccup's neck stick straight up like the
spines on a sea urchin.

Individually, dragons tend to have a healthy
sense of self-preservation, but they are braver when
they hunt in packs. They knew now that they had the
advantage of massive numbers, so they didn't check
their flying for an instant. They just kept on coming.

Gobber let go of the axe.

Spinning end to end, the axe soared up through
the softly falling snow. It hit the biggest dragon of
the lot, killing him instantly, and then carried on going,
landing in a snow-drift hundreds of feet away and
disappearing.

This made the rest of the dragons think a bit.
Some of them scrambled over each other in their
haste to fly away, yelping like dogs. The others came
to a halt, hovering uncertainly, screaming defiance but

keeping their distance.

'Waste of a good axe,' grunted Gobber. 'Keep going, boys, they could come back!'

Hiccup needed no encouragement to keep going. As soon as he got out of the gorge and on to the marshy land behind it, he broke into a stumbling run, every now and then falling flat on his face in the snow.

Some time later, when Gobber reckoned they were a safe distance from Wild Dragon Cliff, he yelled at the boys to stop.

Very carefully he counted heads again, to check he hadn't lost anybody. Gobber had spent an unpleasant ten minutes standing at the mouth of the dragons' cave wondering why there was such a terrible racket and what he was going to say to Stoick the Vast if he lost his precious son and heir for good.

Something Tactful and Sensitive, he supposed, but Tact and Sensitivity were not Gobber's strong points and he took the first five minutes to come up with 'Hiccup copped it. SORRY.' and then spent the second five minutes tearing his beard out.

Consequently, although secretly mightily relieved, he was not in a Good Mood and, as soon as he could get his breath back, he exploded all over the place, as the boys stood, shivering violently, in a bedraggled line.

'NEVER... in FOURTEEN YEARS... have I come across such a load of HOPELESS BARNACLES as you lot. WHICH OF YOU USELESS MOLLUSCS WAS RESPONSIBLE FOR WAKING UP THE DRAGONS????'

'I was,' said Hiccup. Which wasn't strictly true.

'Oh, that's BRILLIANT,' bellowed Gobber, 'just BRILLIANT. Our Future Leader shows off his magnificent Leadership Skills. At the tender age of ten and a half he does his best to annihilate himself and the rest of you in A SIMPLE MILITARY EXERCISE!'

Snotlout sniggered.

'You find something amusing about that, Snotlout?' asked Gobber, with dangerous softness. 'EVERYBODY IS ON LIMPET RATIONS FOR THE NEXT THREE WEEKS.'

The boys groaned.

'Smart work, Hiccup,' sneered Snotlout. 'I can't wait to see you in action on the battlefield.'

'SILENCE!' yelled Gobber. 'THIS IS YOUR

34

INITIATION, NOT A DAY OUT IN THE
COUNTRY! SILENCE, OR YOU'LL BE
LUNCHING ON LUGWORMS FOR THE REST
OF YOUR LIVES!'

'Now,' continued Gobber, more calmly,
'although that was an absolute mess, it wasn't a total
disaster. I PRESUME that you do all HAVE a dragon
after that fiasco…?'

'Yes,' chorused the boys.

Fishlegs took a sideways glance at Hiccup, who
was staring straight ahead.

'Lucky for you,' said Gobber, ominously. 'So you
have all passed the first part of the Dragon Test. There
are, however, still two parts that you have to complete
before you can become full members of the Tribe.
Your next task will be to train this dragon yourself. This
will be a test of the force of your personality. You will
assert your will over this wild creature and show it who
is Master. Your dragon will be expected to obey simple
commands such as "go" and "stay", and hunt fish for
you in the way that dragons have hunted for the Sons
of Thor since anybody can remember. If
you are worried about the training process, you should
study a book called *How To Train Your Dragon* by

Professor Yobbish, which you will find in the fireplace of the Great Hall.'

Suddenly Gobber looked very pleased with himself. 'I stole that book from the Meathead Public Library myself,' he said modestly, regarding his very black fingernails. 'From right under the nose of the Hairy Scary Librarian... He never noticed a thing... Now THAT'S burglary for you...'

Wartihog put up his hand. 'What happens if we can't read, sir?'

'No boasting, Wartihog!' boomed Gobber. 'Get some idiot to read it for you. Your dragons will begin to go back to sleep, because this is still their hibernation time' – some of the dragons had, indeed, gone very quiet inside the baskets – 'so take them home and put them in a warm place. They should wake up in the next couple of weeks. You will then have only FOUR MONTHS to prepare for Initiation Day at the Thor'sday Thursday Celebrations, and the final part of your Test. If, on that day, you can prove that you have trained your dragon to the satisfaction of myself and other elders of the Tribe, you can finally call yourself a Hooligan of Berk.'

The boys stood very tall and tried to look like

proper Hooligans.

'HEROES OR EXILE!' yelled Gobber the Belch.

'HEROES OR EXILE!' yelled eight boys
fanatically back at him.

Exile, thought Hiccup and Fishlegs sadly.

♦ ♦ ♦

'I… hate… being… a… Viking,' panted Fishlegs to
Hiccup as they stumbled back through the bracken
to the Hooligan village.

You didn't really *walk* on the island of Berk, you
waded – through heather or bracken or mud or snow,
that clung on to your legs and made them difficult to
lift. It was the sort of country where the sea and the
land were always falling into one another and getting
mixed up. The island was shot through with holes
burrowed by the water, a maze of criss-crossing
underground streams. You could put your foot on a
solid-looking piece of grass and find yourself
disappearing up to your thigh in black, sticky mud.
You could be making your way through the ferns and
suddenly find yourself fording a river, waist-high
and icy-cold.

The boys were already soaked to the skin with
sea-water, and now the snow had turned to horizontal

driving rain, blowing in their faces with the strength of one of the gale force winds that were always shrieking across the salty wastelands of Berk.

'A narrow escape from horrible death first thing on Thursday morning,' complained Fishlegs, 'followed by complete rejection by the junior half of the Tribe… Nobody's going to talk to me for YEARS after this – except for you, of course, Hiccup, but then you're just a weirdo like me— '

'Thank you,' said Hiccup.

'And on top of everything,' continued Fishlegs bitterly, 'a two-mile run carrying a deranged dragon on my back' – the basket on Fishlegs's back was plunging wildly from side to side as the dragon inside tried manically to get out – 'and only a dinner of horrible

limpets to look forward to at the end of it.'

Hiccup agreed that it wasn't a delicious prospect.

'You can have this dragon back if you like, Hiccup. I warn you, they're filthy heavy when they're wet and cross,' said Fishlegs, miserably. 'Gobber is going to go off like a typhoon when he finds out you haven't got a dragon.'

'But I HAVE got one,' said Hiccup.

Fishlegs stopped and began to take the basket off his back. 'I know it IS yours REALLY,' he sighed wearily. 'I think I'll just go straight past the village and keep on running till I reach somewhere civilised. Rome perhaps. I've always wanted to go to Rome. And I haven't got a hope in Valhalla of passing Initiation anyway, so—'

'No, I've got *another* one, in my basket,' Hiccup insisted.

Fishlegs's jaw dropped open in disbelief.

'I got it when I went back into the tunnel,' explained Hiccup.

'Well, blister my barnacles,' said Fishlegs. 'How in Thor's name did you know it was there? It was so dark you couldn't see the horns in front of you.'

'It was weird,' said Hiccup. 'I sort of sensed it

when we were running down the tunnel. I couldn't see anything, but as we were passing, I just *knew* there was a dragon there, and that it was meant to be MY dragon. I was going to ignore it, actually, because we were in a bit of a hurry but then you said about not having a dragon and I went back, and... there it was, lying on this shelf in the tunnel, just as I'd imagined it would be.'

'Well, jigger my jellyfish,' said Fishlegs, and the boys started running again.

Hiccup was bruised all over, shaking from shock, and he had a nasty dragon-wound in his calf, which was stinging like crazy from the saltwater. He was freezing cold and there was an irritating bit of seaweed in one of his sandals.

He was also a bit worried because he knew he should not have risked his life trying to get a dragon for Fishlegs. This was not the act of a Viking Hero. A Viking Hero would know not to intervene between Fishlegs and his Fate.

On the other hand, Hiccup had been worrying about Dragon-catching Day for longer than he could remember. He had been sure he would be the only one to come back without a dragon, and shame, embarrassment and awful exile would follow.

And now, here he was: a Viking warrior WITH a dragon.

So, on the whole, he was feeling fairly pleased with himself.

Things were looking up.

♥ ♥ ♥

'You know, Hiccup,' said Fishlegs a little later, as the wooden fortifications of the village appeared on the horizon, 'that sounds like Fate, you sensing the dragon was there like that. This could be Meant-To-Be. You could have some sort of wonder-dragon in there. Something that makes a Monstrous Nightmare look like a flying frog! You are the son and heir of Chief Stoick after all, and it's about time Fate came in with a sign about your destiny.'

The boys stopped, puffing with exhaustion.

'Oh, I'm sure it's just a Common or Garden that wandered away from the rest,' said Hiccup, trying to sound careless but unable to keep the excitement out of his voice. *He could have something marvellous in there!*

Maybe Old Wrinkly was right. Old Wrinkly was Hiccup's grandfather on his mother's side. He had

41

taken up soothsaying in his old age and he kept on telling Hiccup how he had looked into the future and that Hiccup was destined for great things.

This amazing dragon could be the beginning of his transformation from ordinary old Hiccup, who wasn't particularly good at anything, into a Hero of the Future!

Hiccup took the basket off his back and paused before opening it.

'It's very still, isn't it?' said Fishlegs, suddenly less certain of the Fate theory. 'I mean, it isn't moving at all in there. Are you sure it's alive?'

'It's just very deeply asleep,' said Hiccup. 'It was stone-cold when I picked it up.'

Suddenly he had a strong feeling that the gods were on his side. He KNEW that this dragon was alive.

With trembling fingers, Hiccup undid the latch, took off the lid of the basket, and peered in. Fishlegs joined him.

Things weren't looking so good any more.

There, curled up fast asleep in the bottom of the basket in a tangled dragon knot, lay perhaps the most common or garden Common or Garden Dragon Hiccup had ever seen.

was how SMALL it was. The most extraordinary thing about this dragon was how SMALL it was.

43

Absolutely the *only* extraordinary thing about this dragon was how extraordinarily SMALL it was. In this it was *truly* extraordinary.

Most dragons that the Vikings used for hunting purposes were about the size of a Labrador dog. The adolescent dragons the boys were collecting weren't quite that big, but they *were* nearly fully-grown. This dragon was more comparable to a West Highland Terrier.

Hiccup couldn't think how he had overlooked this when he picked the dragon up in the tunnel. He supposed, miserably, that it was rather a pressured moment, what with three thousand dragons trying to kill him at the time. And dragons in a deep Sleep Coma do tend to weigh more than they do when they're awake.

'Well,' said Hiccup at last, 'that's a sign, if you like. You reach for a Deadly Nadder and what do you get? A Basic Brown. I grab a dragon in the dark and what do I get? A Common or Garden. The thing is, the gods are telling us we're Common or Garden folk, Fishlegs. You and I, we're not *meant* to be Heroes.'

'It doesn't matter about ME...' said Fishlegs,

'but you *are* meant to be a Hero. Remember? Son of the Chief and all that? And you *will* be one, I know you will…'

Fishlegs put the basket back on Hiccup's back and they trudged towards the village gates together.

'… At least, I sincerely HOPE you will. I don't want to be following Snotlout into battle. You've got more ideas about military tactics in your little finger than Snotlout has in his whole fat head…'

While that may have been true, not only was Hiccup *not* about to be the future star of Dragontraining – but with this particular dragon it was even going to be difficult for him to take his familiar place fading into the background.

It was so small it was going to make him look ridiculous.

It was so small that Snotlout was going to have some very unpleasant things to say about it.

4. HOW TO TRAIN YOUR DRAGON

'HA HA HA HA!'

Snotlout was laughing so hard that he hadn't managed to say anything at all.

The boys were hanging about the village gates, taking the opportunity to show off the dragons that they had caught. Hiccup had tried to walk through without being noticed, but Snotlout had stopped him.

'Let's see what pathetic creature Hiccup has got,' said Snotlout, and took off the lid.

'Oh, this is BRILLIANT – look at it!' said Snotlout, when he finally got his breath back from laughing. 'What IS it, Hiccup? An ickle brown bunny rabbit with wings? A flower fairy? A fluffy flying frog? Gather round everybody and see the magnificent animal that Our Future Leader has caught himself!'

'Oh, Hiccup, you are *useless*,' crowed Speedifist. 'You're the son of a CHIEF, for Thor's sake. Why didn't you get one of those

46

new Monstrous Nightmares with the six-foot wing-span and the extra-extendable claws? They're really mean killers, they are.'

'I have one,' grinned Snotlout, gesturing to the terrifying-looking, flame-red animal fast asleep in his basket. 'I think I shall call her FIREWORM. What are you going to call yours, Hiccup? Sweetums? Sugarlips? Babyface?'

Hiccup's dragon took this particular moment to give a huge yawn, opening his tiny mouth wide to reveal a flickering, forked tongue, very pink gums and ABSOLUTELY NO TEETH AT ALL.

Snotlout laughed so hard, Dogsbreath had to hold him upright.

'TOOTHLESS!' cried Snotlout.
'Hiccup has found himself the only
TOOTHLESS dragon in the uncivilised
world! This is too good. Hiccup the
USELESS and his dragon, TOOTHLESS!'

Fishlegs leapt to Hiccup's defence.

'Well, *you* are not allowed that Monstrous
Nightmare that you've got there, Snotface Snotlout.
Only the son of a Chief is allowed a Monstrous
Nightmare. That Fireworm dragon is Hiccup's, by
right.'

Snotlout's eyes narrowed. He grabbed Fishlegs's
arm and twisted it viciously behind his back.

'Nobody's listening to you, you plankton-
hearted, fish-legged, disaster area,' sneered Snotlout.
'Thanks to you and your snivelling, sneezing disability,
that whole military operation was nearly a total
disaster. When I'm Chief of this Tribe the first thing
I'm going to do is boot anybody with a pathetic allergy
like yours straight out into exile. You're not fit to be a
Hooligan!'

Fishlegs went very white in the face, but he
still managed to gasp out, 'But you are NOT going
to be Chief of this Tribe. HICCUP is going to be

Chief of this Tribe.'

Snotlout dropped Fishlegs's arm and advanced menacingly on Hiccup.

'Oh, he is, is he?' jeered Snotlout. 'So, I'm not allowed that Monstrous Nightmare, am I? Our Future Leader is keeping very quiet about it, isn't he? Come on, Hiccup, I'm stealing your inheritance. What are you going to do about it, then, eh?'

The boys all looked solemn. Snotlout really had broken an ancient Viking rule.

'Hiccup should challenge you for the dragon,' said Fishlegs slowly, and everybody swivelled round to look expectantly at Hiccup.

'Oh, brilliant,' muttered Hiccup under his breath. 'Thank you, Fishlegs. My day just gets better and better.'

Snotlout was a great brute of a boy who didn't really need Dogsbreath's help when it came to bashing people up. He wore specially-constructed, bronze-tipped sandals in order to cause maximum damage when kicking people. Hiccup tried to stay out of his way as much as he possibly could.

But he couldn't ignore this insult to his status, now Fishlegs had helpfully pointed it out, without looking like a coward in front of the other boys. And if you became known as a coward in the Hooligan Tribe, you might as well go the whole hog and wear a pale pink jerkin, take up playing the harp, and change your name to Ermintrude.

'I challenge you, Snotface Snotlout, for the dragon, Fireworm, who is mine by right,' said Hiccup, trying to hide his reluctance by speaking as loudly and formally as he could.

'I accept your challenge,' said Snotlout super-fast, grinning all over his horrid, smug face. 'Axes or fists?'

'Fists,' said Hiccup. Because axes were a REALLY bad idea.

'I shall look forward to showing you how a real Future Hero fights,' said Snotlout, and then he remembered something. 'AFTER the Initiation thing on Thor'sday Thursday, though. I don't want to stub my toe or anything while I'm kicking you all around the village.'

'Hiccup might win,' Fishlegs pointed out.

'OF COURSE he won't win,' boasted Snotlout. 'Look at my sporting ability, my Viking courage, my capacity for mindless violence. I shall win just as surely as I shall be Chief of this Tribe one day. I mean, look at my dragon and then look at HIS dragon.' He pointed mockingly at Toothless. 'The gods have spoken. It's only a matter of time.'

'In the meantime,' Snotlout carried on, 'I shall live in fear of being gummed to death by Hiccup's terrifying, toothless terrapin.'

And Snotlout sauntered off in a lordly fashion, giving Hiccup a nasty kick on the shins as he did so.

♥ ♥ ♥

'Sorry about the challenge,' Fishlegs apologised, after they had left the baskets with the dragons in them under their beds at their homes.

'Oh, don't worry about it,' said Hiccup. 'Somebody would have got me to do it anyway. You know how they all love a fight.'

Fishlegs and Hiccup were going to the Great Hall to look for the book Gobber had recommended: *How to Train Your Dragon*, by Professor Yobbish.

'As it happens,' confided Hiccup, 'I know a bit about dragons already, but I haven't the foggiest clue how to start training one. I would have said they were virtually untrainable. I'm really looking forward to getting some tips.'

The Great Hall was a hullabaloo of young barbarians fighting, yelling, and playing the popular Viking game of Bashyball, which was a very violent contact sport with lots of contact and very few rules.

Hiccup and Fishlegs found the book tucked away in the fireplace, practically in the fire.

Hiccup had never noticed it before.

He opened the book.

(I have included a basic replica of *How to Train Your Dragon*, by Professor Yobbish, here – in order that you can share the experience with Hiccup of opening that book for the first time, full of hope, and interest, and expectation. You will have to imagine that the cover is unusually thick, with huge golden clasps, and that some scribe has covered it in elaborately fancy gilt lettering. It looks very inviting indeed.)

HOW TO TRAIN YOUR DRAGON

—BY—

PROFESSOR YOBBISH

BA, MA Hons, Cantab. Etc.

BIG AXE BOOKS
10th Anniversary Edition

Winner of the
Best Book for Barbarians Gold Award

This book is dedicated to Mummy, with love from your dearest Yob.

The publishers, Big Axe Books Ltd, would like to point out that they take no responsibility whatsoever for any injuries that may occur as a result of any person or persons following the advice given in this book. Thank you for your attention.

BEOWULF is a SOFTY

come heer and say that

MEATHEAD PUBLIC LIBRARY

A note from the Hairy Scary Librarian: Please return this book on or before the last date stamped or I will be VERY ANNOYED. I think you know what I mean.

10 JUNE	789	AD
9 APRIL	835	AD
16 MAY	866	AD

DO NOT REMOVE THIS BOOK OR WE WILL BASH YOU!!!

MY DAD IS TUFFER THAN YOOR

NO WAY ➔ DAD

MY dad cood hav

your dad for brekfast

ABOUT THE AUTHOR

Professor Yobbish (BA, MA Hons, Cantab. etc.) has spent many years in the wild observing dragons in their natural habitat. This book is the culmination of his research and it is the definitive text book on the subject of these fascinating creatures.

Professor Yobbish lives alone in a cave on the Isle of Doom. He is the author of *Looking After Your Killer Whale* and *Sharks and Other Great Pets*. He is currently writing a book about butterflies.

CHAPTER THE FIRST (AND LAST)

The Golden Rule of Dragon-Training is to...

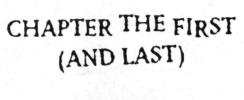

YELL AT IT!

(The louder the better.)

THE END.

How would YOU train a dragon?

Look inside for ALL the answers in Professor Yobbish's hugely entertaining and informative book. Follow his simple advice and you will soon be on your way to becoming the Hero you've always wanted to be...

Praise for *How To Train Your Dragon*:

'This book changed my life.'
Squidface the Terrible

'A brilliant book.' *The Meathead Monthly*

'Nobody yells better than Professor Yobbish. This is a sensitive and well-researched book that contains all the information you need to turn your dragon into a pussy cat.' **The Hooligan** Observer

'Yobbish is a genius.' *The Viking Times*

PRICE: 1 SMALLISH CHICKEN
20 OYSTERS

'THAT'S IT???' said Hiccup furiously, turning the book upside down and shaking it, trying to see whether there was anything other than that single page of paper inside it.

Hiccup put the book down. His face was unusually grim.

'OK, Fishlegs,' he said, 'unless you're any better at yelling than I am, we're on our own. We're going to have to work out our *own* method of dragon-training.'

Stoick the VAST

5. A CHAT WITH OLD WRINKLY

The next morning, Hiccup checked the dragon under his bed. It was still asleep.

When his mother, Valhallarama, asked him at breakfast, 'How did Inititation go yesterday, dear?', Hiccup said, 'Oh, it was fine. I caught my dragon.'

'That's nice, dear,' Valhallarama replied vaguely.

Stoick the Vast looked up briefly from his bowl and boomed, 'EXCELLENT, EXCELLENT,' before getting back to the important task of shovelling food into his mouth.

After breakfast, Hiccup went to sit on the front step beside his grandfather, who was smoking a pipe. It was a beautiful, cold, clear winter's morning, with not a breath of wind and the sea all around as flat as glass.

Old Wrinkly blew out smoke rings contentedly as he watched the sun coming up. Hiccup shivered and chucked stones into the bracken. Neither of them spoke for a long time.

At last Hiccup said, 'I got that dragon.'

'I said you would, didn't I?' replied Old Wrinkly,

very pleased with himself. Old Wrinkly had taken up soothsaying in his old age, mostly unsuccessfully. Looking into the future is a complicated business. So he was particularly pleased that he'd got this right.

'Something extraordinary, you said,' complained Hiccup. 'A truly *unusual* dragon, you said. An animal that would really make me stand out in the crowd.'

'Absolutely,' agreed Old Wrinkly. 'The entrails were undeniable.'

'The *only* extraordinary thing about this dragon,' continued Hiccup, 'is how *extraordinarily* SMALL it is. In that it *is* super-unusual. I'm even more of a laughing-stock than ever.'

'Oh dear,' said Old Wrinkly, chuckling in a wheezy way over his pipe.

Hiccup looked at him reproachfully. Old Wrinkly hurriedly turned the laugh into a cough.

'Size is all relative, Hiccup,' said Old Wrinkly. 'ALL of these dragons are super-small compared to a real Sea Dragon. A REAL Sea Dragon is fifty *times* as big as that little creature. A real Sea Dragon from the bottom of the ocean can swallow ten large Viking ships in one gulp and not even notice.

62

A real Sea Dragon is a cruel, careless mystery like the mighty ocean itself, one moment calm as a scallop, the next raging like an octopus.'

'Well, here on Berk,' said Hiccup, 'where we haven't any Sea Dragons to compare anything with, my dragon is just considerably smaller than everybody else's. You are getting off the point.'

'Am I?' asked Old Wrinkly.

'The point is, I just don't see how I am ever going to become a Hero,' said Hiccup gloomily. 'I am the least Heroic boy in the whole Hooligan Tribe.'

'Oh pshaw, this ridiculous Tribe,' fumed Old Wrinkly. 'OK so you are not what we call a born Hero. You're not big and tough and charismatic like Snotlout. But you're just going to have to work at it. You're going to have to learn how to be a Hero the Hard Way.'

'Anyway,' said Old Wrinkly, 'it might be just what this Tribe needs, a change in leadership style. Because the thing is, times are changing. We can't get away with being bigger and more violent than everybody else any more. IMAGINATION. That's what they need and what you've got. A Hero of the Future is going to have to be clever and cunning, not just a big lump with overdeveloped muscles. He's going to have to stop everyone quarrelling among themselves and get them to face the enemy together.'

'How am I going to persuade anybody to do anything?' asked Hiccup. 'They've started calling me HICCUP THE USELESS. That is not a great name for a Military Leader.'

'You have to see the bigger picture, Hiccup,' continued Old Wrinkly, ignoring him. 'You're called a few names. You're not a natural at Bashyball. Who cares? These are very little problems in the grand scheme of things.'

'It's all very well for you to say they are little problems,' said Hiccup crossly, 'but I have a LOT of little problems. I have to train this super-small dragon in time for Thor'sday Thursday or be thrown out of the Hairy Hooligan Tribe for ever.'

'Ah yes,' said Old Wrinkly, thoughtfully. 'There's a book on this subject, isn't there? Remind me, how does the great Professor of Meathead University think you should train a dragon?'

'He thinks you should yell at it,' said Hiccup, gloomily chucking stones again. 'Show the beast who is Master by the sheer charismatic force of your personality, that sort of thing. I have about as much charisma as a stranded jellyfish and yelling is just another thing I am useless at.'

'Ye-e-es,' said Old Wrinkly, 'but maybe you'll have to Train Your Dragon the Hard Way. You know a very great deal about dragons, don't you, Hiccup? All that Dragon-watching you've been doing over the years?'

'That's a secret,' said Hiccup, uncomfortably.

'I've seen you talking to them,' said Old Wrinkly.

'That's NOT TRUE,' protested Hiccup, going bright-red in the face.

'OK, then,' soothed Old Wrinkly, calmly smoking his pipe, 'it's not true.'

There was silence for a bit.

'It *is* true,' admitted Hiccup, 'but for Thor's sake don't tell

anybody, they wouldn't understand.'

'Talking to dragons is a highly unusual skill,' said Old Wrinkly.

'Maybe,' said Old Wrinkly, 'you can train a dragon better by talking to it, than by yelling at it.'

'That's sweet,' said Hiccup 'and a very touching thought. However, a dragon is not a fluffy creature like a dog or a cat or a pony. A dragon is not going to do what you say just because you ask it pretty please. From what I know about dragons,' said Hiccup, 'I should say that yelling was a pretty good method.'

'But it has its limitations, doesn't it?' Old Wrinkly pointed out. 'I would say that yelling was highly effective on any dragon smaller than a sea-lion. And positively suicidal if you try it on anything larger. Why don't you come up with some alternative training schemes yourself? You might be able to add something to Professor Yobbish's book. I've often thought that that book needs a little something extra... I can't quite put my finger on it...'

'WORDS,' said Hiccup. 'That book needs a lot more words.'

6. MEANWHILE, DEEP IN THE OCEAN...

Meanwhile, deep in the ocean, but not so very far from the Isle of Berk, a real Sea Dragon such as Old Wrinkly had been describing lay sleeping on the sea-bed. He was indescribably large. He had been there so long that he almost seemed to be part of the ocean-floor itself, a great underwater mountain, covered in shells and barnacles, some of his limbs half-buried in the sand.

Generation after generation of little hermit crabs had born and died in this Dragon's ears. Hundreds and hundreds of years he'd slept, because he'd had rather a large meal. He'd had the luck to catch a Roman Legion camping on a cliff-top – they were completely cut off and he had spent an enjoyable afternoon wolfing down the whole lot of them, from commanding officer to lowliest private. Horses, chariots, shield and spears, the entire lot went down the ravenous, reptilian gullet. And, while things such as golden chariot wheels are an additional source of fibre to a Dragon's diet, they do

67

take some time to digest.

The Dragon had crawled down into the depths of the ocean and gone into a Sleep Coma. Dragons can stay in this suspended state for eternity, half-dead, half-alive, buried under fathom after fathom of icy-cold sea-water. Not a muscle of this particular Dragon had moved for six or seven centuries.

But the previous week, a Killer Whale who had chased some seals unexpectedly deep was surprised to notice a slight movement in the upper eyelid of the dragon's right eye. An ancestral memory stirred in the whale's brain and he swam away from there as fast as his fins could carry him. And, a week later, the sea around the Dragon Mountain – which had previously been teeming with crabs and lobsters and shoals and shoals of fish – was a great, underwater desert. Not a mollusc stirred, not a scallop shimmied.

The only sign of life for miles and miles was the rapid jerking of both the Dragon's eyelids, fluttering up and down as if the Dragon had suddenly gone into a lighter sleep and was dreaming, who knows what dark dreams.

7. TOOTHLESS WAKES UP

Toothless woke up about three weeks later. Fishlegs and Hiccup were at Hiccup's house. Everybody else was out, so Hiccup decided to take the opportunity to check on Toothless's basket. He pulled it out from under the bed. A thin plume of bluey-grey smoke was drifting out from under the lid.

Fishlegs whistled. 'He's awake all right,' said Fishlegs. 'Here we go.'

Hiccup opened the basket.

The smoke billowed out and made Hiccup and Fishlegs cough. Hiccup fanned it away. Once his eyes had stopped watering he could make out a very small, ordinary dragon looking up at him with enormous, innocent, grass-green eyes.

'Hello, Toothless*,' said Hiccup, in what he hoped was a good accent in Dragonese.

'What are you doing?' asked Fishlegs curiously. Dragonese is punctuated by shrill shrieks and popping noises and sounds MOST extraordinary when spoken by a human.

---

* This should, of course, read 'Howdeedoodeethere, Toothless,' but I have translated it into English for the benefit of those readers whose Dragonese is a bit rusty. Please read Hiccup's book, *Learning to Speak Dragonese,* for a crash course in this fascinating language.

~LEARNING TO SPEAK DRAGONESE~

Introduction

In order to train your dragon without using the
traditional methods of yelling at it, you must first learn
to speak Dragonese. Dragons are the only other
creatures who speak a language as complicated
and sophisticated as humans.

Here are some common dragon
phrases to get you started:

Nee-ah crappa inna di hoosus, pishyou.
No poo-ing inside the house, please.

Mi Mama no likeit yum-yum on di bum.
My mother does not like to be bitten on the bottom.

Pishyou keendlee gobba oot mi freeundlee?
Please would you be so kind as to spit my friend out?

Doit wummortime.
Let's try that again.

'Just talking to it,' mumbled Hiccup, very embarrassed.

'Just *talking* to it???' gasped Fishlegs, in astonishment. 'What do you *mean*, you're talking to it? You can't talk to it, it's an ANIMAL, for Thor's sake!'

'Oh shut up, Fishlegs,' said Hiccup, impatiently, 'you're frightening it.'

Toothless huffed and puffed and blew out some smoke rings. He inflated his neck to make himself look bigger, which is something dragons do when they are scared or angry.

Eventually he got up the courage to unfurl his wings and flap up on to Hiccup's arm. He walked his way up on to Hiccup's shoulder and Hiccup turned his face towards him.

Toothless pressed his forehead on to Hiccup's forehead and gazed deeply and solemnly into Hiccup's eyes. They stayed there, snout to nose, without moving, for about sixty seconds. Hiccup had to blink a lot because the gaze of a dragon is hypnotic and gives the unnerving feeling that it is sucking your soul away.

Hiccup was just thinking, 'Wow, this is amazing – I'm really making contact here!' when Toothless bent down and bit him on the arm.

Hiccup let out a yelp and threw Toothless off him.

'F-f-fish,' hissed Toothless, hovering in the air in front of Hiccup. 'W-w-w-want fish NOW!'

'I haven't got any fish,' said Hiccup in Dragonese, rubbing his arm. Luckily Toothless didn't have any teeth but dragons have powerful jaws so it was still painful.

Toothless bit him on the other arm. 'F-F-F-FISH!' said Toothless again.

'Are you OK?' asked Fishlegs. 'I can't believe I'm asking this, but what's he saying?'

'He wants to eat,' replied Hiccup, grimly rubbing both arms. He tried to make his voice sound firm but pleasant; to dominate the creature by the sheer force of his personality, as Gobber had said. 'But WE HAVE NO FISH.'

'OK then,' said Toothless. 'Eat c-c-cat.'

He made a lunge for Fiddlesticks, who streaked up the nearest wall with a yowl of terror.

Hiccup just managed to grab Toothless by the tail

72

as he flew off in pursuit. The dragon struggled wildly, shouting 'WANT F-F-FISH NOW! WANT F-F-FOOD NOW! CATS ARE YUMMY WANT FOOD NOW!'

'We don't HAVE any fish,' repeated Hiccup, from between gritted teeth, feeling all his calmness deserting him, 'and you can't eat the cat – I like him.'

Fiddlesticks mewed indignantly from a beam high up in the roof.

They put Toothless in Stoick's bedroom, where there was a mouse problem.

For a while he was happy swooping after the desperately squeaking mice, but then he got bored and started attacking the mattress.

'STOP!' yelled Hiccup, as feathers flew in all directions.

Toothless replied by sicking up the remains of a recently deceased mouse right in the middle of Stoick's pillow.

'Aaaargh!' said Hiccup.

'AAAAAAARGH!' said Stoick the Vast, who entered the room at that very moment.

Toothless launched himself at Stoick the Vast's beard, which he mistook for a chicken.

'Get him off!' said Stoick.

'He doesn't do what I say,' said Hiccup.

'Yell VERY LOUDLY at him,' Stoick shouted, VERY LOUDLY.

Hiccup yelled as loudly as he could. 'Please will you stop eating my father's beard?'

As Hiccup had suspected, Toothless took absolutely no notice whatsoever.

I KNEW I'd be useless at yelling, thought Hiccup gloomily.

'DROPTOTHEFLOORYOUORRRIBLELIT-TLEREPTILE!' yelled Stoick.

Toothless dropped to the floor.

'You see?' said Stoick. '*That's* how to deal with dragons.'

Newtsbreath and Hookfang, Stoick's hunting dragons, came padding into the room. Toothless stiffened as they paced around him, their yellow eyes glinting evily. Each was about the size of a leopard, and they were as delighted by his arrival as a couple of giant cats might be by that of a cute little kitten.

'Greetings, fellow firebreather,' hissed

Newtsbreath, as he gave the wriggling newcomer a
sniff.

'We must wait,' purred Hookfang menacingly,
'until we are alone and then we can give you a
proper welcome.' He gave a vicious swipe at Toothless
with one paw. A claw like a kitchen knife just nicked
Toothless on the rump and the little dragon howled
and jumped into Hiccup's tunic, until only his tail was
poking out of the neck.

'HOOKFANG!' bellowed Stoick.

'My claw slipped,' whined Hookfang.

'GEDDOUTOFHEREBEFOREIMAKEYOUIN-
TOHANDBAGS!' yelled Stoick, and Newtsbreath and
Hookfang slunk out, muttering obscene dragon curses
under their breaths.

'As I was saying,' said Stoick the Vast. 'THAT'S
how to deal with dragons.'

Stoick was looking at Toothless with un-
characteristic anxiety.

'Son,' said Stoick, hoping there might be some
sort of mistake, 'is this dragon *your* dragon?'

'Yes, father,' Hiccup admitted.

'It's very… well… it's very… SMALL, isn't it?'
said Stoick slowly.

Stoick was not an observant person but even *he* could not fail to notice that this dragon really *was* remarkably small.

'… and it hasn't got any teeth.'

There was an awkward silence.

Fishlegs came to Hiccup's rescue.

'That's because it's an unusual breed,' said Fishlegs. 'A unique and… er… violent species called the Toothless Daydream, distant relations of the Monstrous Nightmare, but far more ruthless and so rare they are practically extinct.'

'Really?' Stoick surveyed the Toothless Daydream doubtfully. 'It looks just like a Common or Garden to me.'

'Ahhh, but with respect, Chief,' said Fishlegs, 'that's where you're WRONG. To the amateur eye and, indeed, to its prey, it looks *exactly* like a Common or Garden. But if you look a little closer the characteristic Daydream marking' – Fishlegs pointed to a wart on the end of Toothless's nose – 'marks it out from the more ordinary breed.'

'By Thor, you're right!' said Stoick.

'And it's not just your *average* Toothless Daydream either.' Fishlegs was getting carried away now. 'This particular dragon is of ROYAL BLOOD.'

'No!' said Stoick, very impressed. Stoick was a terrific snob.

'Yes,' said Fishlegs solemnly. 'Your son has only gone and burgled the offspring of King Daggerfangs himself, the reptilian ruler of Wild Dragon Cliff. The Royal Daydreams tend to start out small but they grow into creatures of IMPRESSIVE – even GARGANTUAN – size.'

'Just like you, eh, Hiccup,' said Stoick, giving a great laugh and ruffling his son's hair.

Stoick's tummy gave out a plaintive rumble like a distant underground explosion. 'Time for a little supper, I think. Clear up this mess, will you, boys?'

Stoick strode off, relieved to have had his faith in his son restored.

'Thanks, Fishlegs,' said Hiccup. 'You were inspired.'

'Not at all,' said Fishlegs. 'I owed you one after setting you up for that fight with Snotlout.'

'Father's going to find out at some point anyway though,' said Hiccup gloomily.

'Not necessarily,' said Fishlegs. 'Look at all that talking you were doing with the Toothless Daydream here. That was INCREDIBLE. UNBELIEVABLE. I've never seen anything like it. You'll be training him in next to no time.'

'I was talking to him, all right,' said Hiccup, 'but he didn't listen to a word I said.'

♦ ♦ ♦

When he was going to bed that night, Hiccup didn't want to leave Toothless in front of the fire with Newtsbreath and Hookfang.

'Can I take him to bed with me?' he asked Stoick.

78

'A dragon is a working animal,' said Stoick the Vast. 'Too much hugging and kissing will make him lose his vicious streak.'

'But Newtsbreath will kill him if I leave him alone with them.'

Newtsbreath gave an appreciative growl. 'It would be my pleasure,' he hissed.

'Nonsense,' boomed Stoick, unaware of Newtsbreath's last remark, as he didn't speak Dragonese. He gave Newtsbreath a friendly cuff round the horns. 'Newtsbreath just wants to play. That sort of rough and tumble is good for a young dragon. Makes him learn to stick up for himself.'

Hookfang extended his claws like flick-knives and drummed them on the hearth.

Hiccup pretended to say goodnight to Toothless by the fire, but smuggled him into the bedroom under his tunic.

'You must be absolutely quiet,' he told Toothless sternly as they climbed into bed, and the dragon nodded eagerly. In fact, he snored loudly the entire night, but Hiccup didn't care. Hiccup spent the whole of the winter on Berk in various states of 'very cold', ranging from 'fairly chilly' to 'absolutely freezing'. At night, too many layers were considered sissy, so Hiccup generally lay awake for a couple of hours until he had shivered himself into a light sleep.

Now though, as Hiccup stretched his feet out against Toothless's back, he felt waves of heat coming off the little dragon, gradually creeping up his legs and warming his freezing cold stomach and heart, even travelling right up to his head, which hadn't been *truly* warm for almost six months. Even his ears burned contentedly. It would have taken the snoring of six strong dragons to have woken Hiccup, so deeply did he sleep that night.

8. TRAINING YOUR DRAGON THE HARD WAY

Hiccup was still pretty certain, knowing dragons as he did, that yelling was the easiest method of training them. So, over the next couple of weeks, he tried yelling at Toothless to see if he could make it work. He tried yelling loudly, firmly, strictly. He looked as cross as he could. But Toothless wouldn't take him seriously.

Hiccup finally gave up on the yelling when Toothless stole a kipper off his plate one morning at breakfast. Hiccup let out his most fierce and frightening yell and Toothless just gave him a wicked look and knocked everything else on to the floor with one swipe of his tail.

That was it with the yelling, as far as Hiccup was concerned.

'OK, then,' said Hiccup, 'I'll try going to the other extreme.'

So he was as nice to Toothless as he possibly could be. He gave Toothless the comfiest bit of the bed and then lay dangerously balanced on the edge of it himself.

He fed him as much kipper and lobster as he wanted. He only did this once, though, as the little dragon just went on eating until he had made himself thoroughly sick.

He played games with him for hours and hours. He told him jokes, he brought him mice to eat, he scratched the bit that Toothless couldn't quite reach in between the spokes on his back.

He made that dragon's life as close to Dragon Heaven as he possibly could.

♦ ♦ ♦

By mid February, the winter was coming to an end on Berk, and the snowy season had turned into the rainy season. It was the kind of weather where your clothes never got dry, no matter what. Hiccup would hang up his sodden tunic on a chair in front of the fire before going to bed at night, and in the morning it would *still* be wet – warm and wet rather than cold and wet, but WET nonetheless.

The ground all around the Village had turned into knee-deep mud.

'What, in Woden's name, are you doing?' asked Fishlegs, when he came across Hiccup digging a large hole just outside the house.

'Building a mud-wallow for Toothless,' panted Hiccup.

'You spoil that dragon, you really do,' said Fishlegs, shaking his head.

'It's psychology, you see,' said Hiccup, 'It's clever and it's subtle, not like that caveman yelling you're doing with Horrorcow.'

Fishlegs had named his dragon Horrorcow. The 'horror' bit was to make the poor creature at least sound a bit frightening. The 'cow' bit was because for a dragon she really *was* remarkably like a cow. She was a large, peaceful, brown creature, with an easy-going nature. Fishlegs suspected she might even be vegetarian.

'I'm always catching her nibbling at the woodwork,' he complained. 'BLOOD, Horrorcow, BLOOD – that's what you should want!'

Nonetheless, maybe Fishlegs *was* a better yeller than Hiccup, or maybe Horrorcow was a lazier and more obliging character than Toothless, but Horrorcow was proving very easy to train by the yelling method.

'OK, Toothless, it's ready,' said Hiccup. 'Get yourself a good wallow.'

83

Toothless stopped trying to catch voles and leapt into the mud. He rolled over and over in the oozy gunge, spreading out his wings and squirming happily.

'I'm bonding with him,' said Hiccup, 'so he'll want to do what I say.'

'Hiccup,' said Fishlegs, as Toothless sucked up a good mouthful of the mud and spat it out straight into Hiccup's face, 'I may not know much about dragons, but I *do* know that they are the most selfish creatures on earth. No dragon is ever going to do what you want out of gratitude. Dragons do not know what gratitude is. Give up. This will NEVER WORK.'

'The thing about us d-d-dragons,' said Toothless, helpfully, 'is we're s-s-survivors. We're not like s-s-soppy cats or d-d-dumb dogs, falling in l-l-love with their Masters and yucky things like that. Only reason we ever do what a m-m-man wants is

84

because he's b-b-bigger than us and gives us food.'

'What's he saying?' asked Fishlegs.

'Pretty much what you're saying,' said Hiccup.

'N-n-never trust a dragon,' said Toothless, cheerfully hopping out of the wallow and helping himself to one of the winkles that Hiccup had found for him. (Toothless was particularly fond of winkles – 'J-j-just like picking your n-n-nose,' he said). 'That's what my m-m-mother taught me in the nest, and she should know.'

Hiccup sighed. It was true. Toothless was cute to look at, and very good company – if a little demanding. However, you only had to look into his big, innocent, heavily-lashed eyes to realise that he was totally without morals. The eyes were ancient, the eyes of a killer. You might as well ask a crocodile or a shark to be your friend.

Hiccup wiped the mud off his face.

'I'll think of something else,' said Hiccup.

♦ ♦ ♦

February turned into March and Hiccup was still thinking. A few flowers made the mistake of appearing and were immediately blasted out of existence by a couple of hard frosts that had kept themselves back for this very purpose.

Fishlegs could now get Horrorcow to 'go' and 'stay' on command. Hiccup was still struggling to teach Toothless the basics of toilet-training.

'NO POOING IN THE KITCHEN,' said Hiccup for the hundredth time, carrying Toothless outside after yet another accident.

'Is w-w-warmer in the kitchen,' whined Toothless.

'But poos go OUTSIDE, you KNOW that,' said Hiccup, at the end of his tether.

Toothless promptly pooed all over Hiccup's hands and down his tunic.

'Is OUTSIDE, is OUTSIDE, is OUTSIDE,' crowed Toothless.

At this inopportune moment, Snotlout and Dogsbreath came sauntering past Stoick's house on the way back from the beach, their dragons on their shoulders.

'Well, well, well,' sneered Snotlout, 'if it isn't the USELESS, covered in dragon poo. It actually quite suits you.'

'Hur, Hur, Hur,' snorted Dogsbreath.

'That's not a dragon,' jeered Seaslug,

86

Dogsbreath's dragon, who was an ugly great Gronckle with a pug nose and a mean temper, 'that's a newt with wings.'

SEASLUG

'That's not a dragon,' scoffed Fireworm, Snotlout's dragon, who was as big a bully as her master, 'that's an ickle newborn bunny wabbit with a pathetic poo problem.'

Toothless gave a gasp of fury.

Snotlout showed Hiccup the immense heap of fish that he had wrapped up in his cloak.

'Look what Fireworm and Seaslug caught down at the beach. And it only took a couple of hours…'

Fireworm coughed, flexed a shining muscle or two and looked at her claws in fake modesty.

'Oh, please,' she drawled. 'I wasn't even CONCENTRATING. If I was TRYING, I could do it in ten minutes, with one wing tied behind my back.'

'Excuse me while I throw up,' muttered Toothless to Horrorcow, who was regarding Fireworm with disapproval in her big brown eyes.

'We reckon Fireworm could be a bit of a

Fireworm

HUNTING LEGEND,' grinned Snotlout. 'I hear that Horrorcow is partial to carrots... Has the Toothless Wonder got up the nerve to attack a vegetable? Carrots are a bit crunchy but perhaps he could manage the odd squished cucumber... You could give it to him through a straw perhaps...'

'HUR, HUR, HUR.' Dogsbreath laughed so hard that snot came snorting out of his nose.

'Careful, Dogsbreath,' said Fishlegs politely, 'your brains are coming out.'

Dogsbreath bashed him hard and the two boys swaggered off, Fireworm making a lunge at Toothless that nearly took his eye out as he went past.

As soon as they were safely out of earshot, Toothless jumped out of Hiccup's arms and coughed out sheets of flame in a menacing manner.

'Bullies! Yellowbellies! Come closer and Toothless'll fry you to a frazzle! Toothless'll drag out yer guts and play 'em on a harp! Toothless'll... Toothless'll... Toothless'll... well, you just better not come any closer that's all...!'

'Oh, very brave,' said Hiccup sarcastically. 'If you shout louder they might even hear you.'

9. FEAR, VANITY, REVENGE AND SILLY JOKES

March turned into April and April turned into May. After Fireworm's remark about the pathetic bunny rabbit, Toothless never pooed in the kitchen again. But Hiccup hadn't made any further progress in training him.

It was still raining, but it was a warm rain. The wind was blowing, but it was a less furious wind. It was just about possible to stand upright.

The gulls' eggs were hatching on the rocks and the parent gulls dive-bombed Hiccup and Fishlegs when they came to the Long Beach to practice.

'KILL, Horrorcow, KILL,' said Fishlegs to Horrorcow, who was calmly perched on his shoulder. 'You could have that Black-backed Gull for breakfast, he's barely half your size. Honestly, Hiccup, I give up, I don't know how I'm going to pass the hunting section of the test, Horrorcow just doesn't have the killer instinct. She'd never survive in the wild.'

Hiccup laughed hollowly. 'You think YOU'VE got problems? Toothless and I are failing right from the beginning: the basic obedience commands,
the retrieval, the compulsory exercises, the hunting – the lot.'

'It can't be *that* bad,' said Fishlegs.

'Watch,' said Hiccup.

The boys moved along the beach a bit, out of range of the gulls.

They started practising the most basic command of all: 'go'. The dragon was supposed to stand, bolt upright, on the handler's outstretched arm. The handler would then bark the command as loudly as possible, while simultaneously lifting his arm to fling the dragon into the air. The dragon was supposed to soar gracefully into flight when the handler's arm reached its highest point.

Horrorcow yawned, scratched and slowly flapped off, grumbling to herself.

Toothless was even less obedient.

'GO!' yelled Hiccup.

Hiccup flung his arm up. Toothless hung on.

'I said GO!' Hiccup repeated in frustration.

Toothless would not budge...

'W-w-why g-g-go?' shuddered Toothless, gripping even tighter.

'Just go GO GO GO GO!!!!' screamed Hiccup, flapping his arm up and down frantically, with Toothless hanging on to it for dear life.

Toothless stayed.

'Toothless,' said Hiccup, as reasonably as he could, 'please go. If you don't start going when I tell you to, we are both going to be thrown into exile.'

'But I don't w-w-want to go,' Toothless pointed

out, equally reasonably.

Fishlegs watched the whole process in appalled amazement. 'You really *do* have problems,' he said in an awed voice.

'Yup,' said Hiccup. He finally managed to uncurl Toothless's claws, which had relaxed their grip for a second, and pushed him off. Toothless landed on the sand with a squeal of outrage, and immediately attached himself to Hiccup's leg, getting a good grip on the sandals with his talons, and wrapping his wings around Hiccup's calf.

'N-n-not going,' said Toothless stubbornly.

'It can't get much worse than this,' said Hiccup, 'so I'm going to try a new tack.' He took out the notebook in which he had been jotting down all he knew about dragons in the hope that it might be useful. 'DRAGON MOTIVATION…' Hiccup read aloud, '1. GRATITUDE.' Hiccup sighed. '2. FEAR. That works, but I can't do it. 3, 4, 5, GREED, VANITY and REVENGE. Those are all worth a try. 6. JOKES AND RIDDLING TALK. Only if I'm desperate.'

'This has got to be a first,' drawled Fishlegs, 'but I'm with Gobber the Belch on this one. Why don't you just yell a bit louder?'

Hiccup

DRAGON MOTIVASHUN

1. ~~GRATITUDE~~ Dragons are never~~,~~~~x~~
grateful

2. ~~FEAR~~. Works but I cant do it.
✗

3. ~~GREED~~ Coud fill him up
so much he can't fly ? ✗

4. VANITTY. Possible.

5. Revenge ??? Worth a try

6. JOKES AND RIDDLING TALK.
↑
only if I'm desparate.

THE MONSTROUS NIGHTMARE

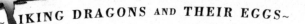

The Monstrous Nightmare is a terrifying domestic dragon. Dazzling flyers, magnificent hunters and fearsome fighters, they can be wild and difficult to train. By unofficial Viking Law, only a Chief or the son of a Chief can own one.

~ STATISTICS ~

COLOURS: Emerald green, brilliant scarlet, deepest purple.

ARMED WITH: Scary fangs, extra extendable claws.

FEAR FACTOR:......... 6

ATTACK:................... 7

SPEED:..................... 9

SIZE:....................... 5

DISOBEDIENCE:........ 3

Hiccup ignored him.

'OK, Toothless,' said Hiccup to the little dragon, who was pretending to be asleep as he held on to Hiccup's leg. 'For every fish you catch me I will give you two more lobsters when you get home.'

Toothless opened his eyes. 'A-a-alive?' he said eagerly. 'C-c-can Toothless kill them? P-p-please? Just this once?'

'No, Toothless,' said Hiccup, firmly, 'I keep on telling you, it isn't kind to torture creatures smaller than yourself.'

Toothless closed his eyes again. 'You're so b-b-boring,' he said sulkily.

'You're such a clever, quick dragon, Toothless,' Hiccup flattered, 'I bet you could catch more fish than any of the others on Thor'sday Thursday if you wanted to.'

Toothless opened his eyes to consider the matter. 'T-t-twice as many,' he said modestly. 'But I don't w-w-want to.'

This was unanswerable. Hiccup crossed VANITY off his list.

'You know that big red Fireworm dragon who was so rude to you?' said Hiccup.

Toothless spat on the ground in indignation. 'S-s-said I was a newt with wings. S-s-said I was an incontinent bunny r-r-rabbit. T-t-toothless going to k-k-kill her. Toothless going to s-s-scratch her to death. T-t-toothless going to—'

'Yes, yes, yes,' said Hiccup hastily. 'That Fireworm dragon and her master who looks like a pig think that Fireworm is going to catch more fish than anybody else at the Thor'sday Thursday celebrations. Think how stupid they are going to look if YOU win the prize for Most Promising Dragon instead of her.'

Toothless got off Hiccup's leg. 'I W-W-WILL think about that,' said Toothless. He waddled off a couple of feet and thought about it.

Five minutes later he was still thinking. He let out the odd chuckle every now and then, but every time Hiccup said, 'So, how about it, then?' he just replied, 'S-s-still thinking. Go away.'

With a sigh, Hiccup put a line through REVENGE.

'OK,' said Fishlegs, looking over Hiccup's shoulder. 'You've tried everything else. How about JOKES AND RIDDLING TALK? I assume you are desperate.'

'Toothless,' said Hiccup. 'If you catch me a nice big mackerel you will be the cleverest, fastest dragon on Berk AND you will make that Fireworm dragon look like an idiot AND you will have all the lobsters you can eat when we get home AND I will tell you a really good joke.'

Toothless turned round. 'T-t-toothless loves jokes.' He flapped on to Hiccup's arm again. 'All right. Toothless help you. B-b-but NOT because me being n-n-nice or anything yucky...'

'No, no,' said Hiccup. 'Of course not.'

'Us d-d-dragons cruel and mean. But we do love a j-j-joke. Tell me NOW.'

Hiccup laughed. 'No way. AFTER you bring me a mackerel.'

'OK, then,' said Toothless.

He jumped off Hiccup's arm into the air.

A dragon hunting is a very impressive sight, even a scrawny infant one like Toothless. He flew across the beach in his usual, untidy, lopsided fashion, shrieking a few insults along the way at any cormorants that looked smaller than him. But as soon as he reached the sea, Toothless seemed to grow up a bit. The sea-salt awoke in him some ancestral memory of the great

97

pedigree hunting monsters that were his forefathers. He spread out his wings like a kite and flew fairly swiftly over the surface of the choppy waves, keeping his body and wings steady as he searched for the movement of fish. He spotted something, and soared upwards in circles until he was so high that Hiccup, craning his neck backwards on the beach, could only just see him as a tiny speck. The speck was motionless for a second, and then Toothless dived, his wings folded by his sides, dropping like a stone out of the sky.

He disappeared into the water and was gone for quite a while. Dragons can stay underwater for at least five minutes, if they want to, and Toothless got quite distracted under there, chasing one fish and then another, unable to decide which was the biggest.

Hiccup had got bored, and was looking for oysters, when Toothless came bursting triumphantly out of the sea carrying a small mackerel.

He dropped the mackerel at Hiccup's feet, did three somersaults in a row and landed on Hiccup's head. He let out the dragon's cry of triumph, which is a bit like a rooster crowing but a lot louder and more self-satisfied.

Then he leant over and stared
into Hiccup's eyes, upside down.

'Now t-t-tell me a joke,' said Toothless.

'Whimpering Wodens,' said Hiccup. 'He did it.
He really did it.'

'T-t-tell me a JOKE,' said Toothless again.

'What's black and white and red all over?'
asked Hiccup.

Toothless didn't know.

'A sunburnt penguin,' replied Hiccup.

It was a very, very old joke, but apparently it
hadn't made it to Wild Dragon Cliff. Toothless thought
it was hysterically funny.

He flew off to catch more fish so he could hear
more jokes.

It was an enjoyable afternoon. The rain stopped,
the sun shone, and Toothless didn't do too badly at all
with the hunting. He dropped a few fish and, at one
point, wandered off entirely to chase rabbits on the
clifftops. But he came back when Hiccup called,
eventually, and by the end of a couple of hours he had
caught six medium-sized mackerel and a dogfish.

All in all, Hiccup was pretty satisfied.

'After all,' he said to Fishlegs, 'it's not like I'm

expecting to win the prize for Most Promising Dragon
or anything. All I need is to show that Toothless is
basically under my control and for him to catch a
few fish. We'll make fools of ourselves compared to
Snotlout and his beastly Hunting Legend, but at least
we'll have passed Initiation.'

What was more, as Toothless dropped the last
mackerel on the heap in front of Hiccup, Fishlegs
noticed something sharp and gleaming in the dragon's
lower jaw.

'Toothless has got his first tooth!' said Fishlegs.

It seemed a very good omen.

♥ ♥ ♥

As they staggered home they passed Old Wrinkly, who
had been sitting on a rock watching them for the past
couple of hours.

'Ve-ry impressive,' wheezed Old Wrinkly, as the boys showed him the fish wrapped up in Hiccup's cloak.

'We reckon Hiccup really might pass the Final Initiation Test on Thor'sday Thursday,' said Fishlegs excitedly.

'So you're still worrying about that piddly little Test, are you, Hiccup?' asked Old Wrinkly. 'There are larger concerns you know. There's a gi-normous storm brewing up for instance. It should hit us in about three days.'

'Piddly little Test?' said Fishlegs indignantly. 'What do you mean, piddly little Test??? The Thor'sday Thursday Festival is the biggest event of the year. EVERYBODY who is ANYBODY will be there, all the Hairy Hooligans AND the Meatheads. Plus, this may not seem important to YOU, but anybody who fails this piddly little Test gets put into exile to get eaten up by cannibals or something equally gruesome.'

'I'm going to call myself HICCUP THE USEFUL and his dragon TOOTHFULL,' said Hiccup, beaming. 'I thought of it just now and I'm really pleased with it. It's solid, dependable, not too flash and not too much to live up to.'

'This reptile finally got his act together and caught some fish,' said Fishlegs, pointing at Toothless who was picking his nose with one claw. 'Incredible though it may seem, Hiccup may pass this Test after all.'

'Oh, I think it's almost a certainty,' said Old Wrinkly, looking at Toothless, who was now attempting to cross his eyes and falling down in the process.

'Al-most,' repeated Old Wrinkly thoughtfully.

And the boys went home, with Toothless following behind them whining, 'Oh C-C-CARRY ME, CARRY ME... it's not f-f-fair... my wings ache...'

10. THOR'SDAY THURSDAY

The Thor'sday Thursday Celebrations were a truly
spectacular occasion. The Hairy Hooligans' fierce
rivals, the Meatheads, from the nearby Meathead
Islands, sailed across the Inner Ocean to the Isle of
Berk for this great gathering.

The visitors set up camp in Black Heart Bay,
which turned overnight from an empty desert of
echoing seagulls into a bustling village of tents made
out of sails too patched to be used at sea anymore.

By the next morning The Long Beach was
packed with stalls and jugglers and fortune tellers.
There was a happy confusion of Vikings spotting old
friends, and practising their sword play, and yelling at
the children to stop hitting each other RIGHT NOW
for Thor's sake no I REALLY MEAN IT this time…
or… or… or… ELSE.

Vast Viking men sat on uncomfortable rocks

WELCOME TO THE
THOR'SDAY THURSDAY CELEBRATION

- - - -

Programme of events

- - - -

9.00 Hammer-throwing for the Over-60s only.
Meet up at the Marooner's Rock with
your own hammer or somebody else's
(hard hats essential for spectators).

-

**10.30 How Many Gull's Eggs Can
You Eat in One Minute?**
Baggybum the Beerbelly is the
defending champion in this
hotly-contested competition.

-

11.30 Ugliest Baby Contest

-

12.30 Axe-fighting Display
Admire the delicate art of fighting with axes.

-

2.00 Young Heroes Final Initiation Test
Watch tomorrow's Viking Heroes as they compete.
Whose dragon will be the most obedient, and whose
will catch the most fish? Blood, teeth, loud yelling –
this sport has everything.

-

3.30 Grand Raffle and Closing Ceremony

guffawing loudly like gigantic sea-lions in a holiday mood. Impressively large Viking women huddled in groups cackling like seagulls and downing whole mugs of tea in one swallow.

Despite Old Wrinkly's gloomy forecasts of terrible storms and typhoons, it was a gloriously hot June day with not even a hint of a cloud in the offing.

The Young Heroes Final Inititiation Test would not start until 2 p.m. that afternoon, so Hiccup spent the morning listening round-eyed to storytellers telling tall tales of Dirty Danes and pirate princesses.

He was sick with nerves, so found it difficult to enjoy the occasion as much as he had done in previous years.

Even Gobber throwing up during the How Many Gulls Eggs Can You Eat in One Minute? competition failed to raise more than a faint smile on his pale, tense face.

Hiccup's family had a picnic lunch overlooking the Axe-fighting Display. Hiccup could not eat a thing, and nor, unusually, could Toothless, who was in a difficult mood and turned his nose up at the tuna sandwich Valhallarama offered.

'Good to keep your dragon's appetite sharp for the game,' boomed Stoick the Vast, who was in an excellent mood. He had won a bet on Goggletoad in the Ugliest Baby Contest and was looking forward to seeing his son's brilliant display during the Initiation Test.

As the day wore on, a hot wind suddenly started blowing out of nowhere. It was still sweltering, but ominous grey clouds were gathering on the horizon. There was the odd rumble of thunder in the air.

Maybe Old Wrinkly had been right, thought Hiccup as he gazed upwards, and Thor *was* going to put in his traditional appearance at the Thor'sday Thursday celebrations.

'P-P-P-P-A-R-P! Will all youths hoping to be initiated into the Tribes this year please make their way to the ground at the left of the beach.'

Hiccup gulped, nudged Toothless, and stood up. This was it.

♥ ♥ ♥

Hiccup was one of the last to get to the ground, which was a large area of wet sand just at the edge of the sea. The boys from his own Tribe were already assembled, their dragons hovering a couple of couple

of feet above them. Everybody was chattering
excitedly and even Snotlout was looking nervous.

The Meathead boys and their dragons seemed to
be gigantic, rough-looking customers, far tougher than
the Hooligans. One in particular was a great hulking
brute of a boy, who looked fifteen at least.

Thuggory the Meathead and his dragon
KILLER

Hiccup presumed he was Thuggory, Chief Mogadon the Meathead's son, because a silver-grey Monstrous Nightmare about three feet tall was perched on one of his shoulders. It was looking at Fireworm like a Rottweiler thinking evil thoughts.

Fireworm acted unconcerned.

'An aristocrat never growls,' purred Fireworm sweetly. 'You must be one of those mongrel Nightmares. We pure greenbloods descended from the great Ripperclaw himself would never *dream* of doing anything so common.'

The silver Nightmare's growling increased in volume.

The crowd was assembling at the touchline. Hiccup tried not to notice Stoick the Vast blasting his way to the front with great cries of, 'Out of my way, I'm a CHIEF.

'TEN TO ONE MY SON CATCHES MORE FISH THAN YOUR SON IN THIS TEST,' boomed Stoick, giving his old enemy Mogadon the Meathead a good prod in the stomach.

Mogadon the Meathead narrowed his eyes and wondered whether to hit him. Maybe AFTER the Test.

'And which,' asked Mogadon the Meathead, 'is your son? Is he the tall one who looks like a pig with the skeleton tattoos and the red Monstrous Nightmare?'

'Nope,' said Stoick happily. 'That's my brother Baggybum's son. **MY SON** is that skinny one over there with the Toothless Daydream.'

Mogadon the Meathead broke into a big smile.

He slapped Stoick on the back and yelled, **'I TAKE YOUR BET AND DOUBLE IT!'**

'DONE!' shouted Stoick and the two great chieftains shook hands and bumped bellies on the bet.

♥ ♥ ♥

Gobber the Belch was in charge of this final stage of the Initiation Test. He was still looking a bit green from his unpleasant experience in the How Many Gulls' Eggs Can You Eat in One Minute? competition. This had not improved his temper.

'ALL RIGHT, YOU 'ORRIBLE LOT!' yelled Gobber. 'This is where we find out if you are the stuff that Heroes are made of. You will either walk out of this arena full members of the noble Tribes of Hairy Hooligans and Merciless Meatheads OR go into miserable exile for ever from the Inner Isles. Let's see which it's going to be, shall we?'

He grinned nastily at the twenty boys standing before him.

'I shall begin by inspecting you and your animals, as if you were warriors about to go into battle. I shall introduce you to the watching members of the Tribes you hope to enter. Then the Test will begin. You will demonstrate how you have asserted yourselves over these wild creatures and tamed them by the sheer force of your Heroic Personalities.

'You will start by performing the basic commands of "go", "stay" and "fetch". You will end by ordering your reptile to hunt fish for you, as your forefathers have done before you.'

Hiccup swallowed nervously.

'The boy and dragon who most impress the judge, and that is ME,' – Gobber bared his teeth grimly – 'will receive the extra glory of being called the Hero of Heroes and Most Promising Dragon. The boys and dragons who FAIL this Test will say farewell to their families for ever and leave the Tribe to go, where we do not care.' Gobber paused.

'Poetry,' muttered Fishlegs, just loud enough for Gobber to hear. Gobber glared at him.

'HEROES OR EXILES!' yelled Gobber the Belch.

'HEROES OR EXILES!' yelled eighteen boys fanatically back at him.

'HEROES OR EXILES!' yelled the watching Hooligan and Meathead Tribes.

Please let me be a bit of a Hero, just this once, Hiccup and Fishlegs each thought to themselves. Nothing too spectacular or anything, just to get through this Test.

'STAND TO ATTENTION, WITH YOUR DRAGONS ON YOUR RIGHT ARMS!' yelled Gobber the Belch.

Gobber walked down the row of boys for the inspection.

'Beautiful turnout.' Gobber congratulated Thuggory the Meathead on his Nightmare dragon, Killer, who spread out his shining wings to show off a wingspan of about four foot.

Gobber stopped abruptly when he got to Hiccup.

'And WHAT in the name of Woden,' demanded Gobber, blanching a little, 'is THIS?'

'It's a Toothless Daydream, sir,' muttered Hiccup.

'Small but vicious,' added Fishlegs, helpfully.

'Toothless Daydream???' blustered Gobber. 'That's the smallest Common or Garden I have ever seen. What do you think I am, an idiot?'

'No, no, sir,' murmured Fishlegs reassuringly, 'just a little on the slow side.'

Gobber glowered dangerously.

'A Toothless Daydream,' explained Hiccup, 'looks exactly like a Common or Garden except for the characteristic wart on the end of its nose.'

'SILENCE!' said Gobber, in a very loud whisper. 'Or I shall throw you all the way to the Mainland. I HOPE,' he continued, 'that this dragon hunts better than it looks. You and your fishy friend here are the worst candidates for Initiation I have ever had the displeasure of teaching. But you are the future of this Tribe, Hiccup, and if you shame us in front of the Meatheads, I, personally, will never forgive you. Do you understand?'

Hiccup nodded.

112

Each boy then stepped forward to bow and hold up his dragon for the spectators to applaud.

There was huge clapping for Snotface Snotlout and his dragon, Fireworm, only rivalled by the mighty cheering for Thuggory the Meathead and his dragon, Killer.

'I give you, last but not least,' Gobber the Belch was trying to put a bit of enthusiasm into his yelling, 'the fearsome… the terrible… the only son of Stoick the Vast… HICCUP THE USEFUL AND HIS DRAGON TOOTHFULL!'

Hiccup stepped forward and held up Toothless as high as he could to make him look a bit bigger.

There was a slightly appalled silence.

People had seen dragons this small before, of course, normally scampering about after field mice in the wild, but NOT as noble hunting dragons competing in Initiation.

'SIZE ISN'T EVERYTHING!' boomed Stoick, so loudly that you could have heard him several beaches away, and he banged his great hands together to start the applause.

Everyone was terrified of Stoick's famous temper, so they joined in with polite wild cheering.

Toothless was still in a mood, but he was delighted to be the centre of attention, and he puffed out his chest and bowed solemnly to left and right.

A few of the Meatheads sniggered.

I've changed my mind, thought Hiccup, closing his eyes, THIS is the worst moment of my life so far.

'OK, Toothless,' he whispered into the little dragon's ear, 'this is our Big Chance. Catch lots of fish here and I will tell you more jokes than you have ever heard in your life. Which will make that big red Fireworm dragon *really* cross.'

Toothless took a sideways glance at Fireworm. She was sharpening her nails on Snotlout's helmet with the smug certainty of a dragon who knows she's about to win the prize for Most Promising Dragon.

'P-P-PARP!'

The Test began.

♦ ♦ ♦

Toothless didn't do too badly in the early obedience exercises, though he clearly thought it was extremely dull. It was now raining quite hard and Toothless hated the rain. He wanted to go home and relax in front of a nice warm fire.

Fireworm and Killer were 'going' and 'fetching'

as soon as Snotlout and Thuggory commanded, and they were diving and breathing out fire as they did so, just to show off. Fireworm did some fancy acrobatic somersaults that had the crowd screaming and stamping their feet.

'START YOUR HUNTING!' yelled Gobber the Belch.

Every dragon except Toothless flew out to sea.

Toothless flapped back to Hiccup's shoulder.

'T-T-Toothless got a t-t-tummy-ache,' he complained. Hiccup tried not to see his father looking surprised on the sidelines. He tried not to notice the crowd whispering to each other: 'That's Stoick's son over there – no, not the tall one with the skeleton tattoos who looks like a pig, the small skinny one who can't even control his minuscule dragon.'

Toothless got a tummy-ache.

'Don't forget, Toothless,' said Hiccup through gritted teeth, 'the FISH. I'm going to tell you all the jokes I've ever heard, remember?'

'T-t-tell me NOW,' said Toothless.

Help came from an unexpected quarter.

Snotlout broke off from yelling 'KILL, FIREWORM, KILL,' to lean over and sneer at Hiccup. 'What ARE you doing, Hiccup? You're not TALKING to that newt with wings, are you? Talking to dragons is against the rules and forbidden by order of Stoick the Vast, your soppy father…'

'N-n-newt with wings?' repeated Toothless. 'N-N-NEWT WITH WINGS???'

'You're not a newt with wings, are you, Toothless?' said Hiccup. 'You're the best hunter in the world, aren't you?'

'Too RIGHT I am,' said Toothless, grumpily.

'You SHOW that Snotface Snotlout and his snobby dragon what a REAL hunting dragon can do,' said Hiccup urgently.

'OK, then,' said Toothless.

Hiccup heaved a huge sigh of relief as Toothless took off in shambolic fashion in the general direction of the sea.

'This is too good to be true,' Hiccup said to himself ten minutes later as Toothless returned from a second trip, clearly too bored for words but dropping a couple of herring at Hiccup's feet. 'In about half an hour, I, Hiccup, will become a fully paid-up member of the Hairy Hooligan tribe.'

It *was* too good to be true. Fireworm was just flying back to Snotlout with her twentieth fish, her green cat's eyes snapping with triumph, when Toothless called out:

'S-s-sloppy snob.'

Fireworm stopped in mid-air. Her head whipped round, her eyes narrowing.

'WHAT did you say?' hissed Fireworm.

'Oh no,' said Hiccup. 'No, Toothless, no, don't do it...'

'S-s-sloppy snob,' jeered Toothless. 'Is that the best you can do? It's p-p-pathetic. Hopeless. U-u-useless. You N-N-Nightmares think you're so cruel but you're s-s-sloppy as scallops.'

'YOU,' hissed Fireworm, her ears dangerously back as she crept forward through the air like a leopard about to spring, 'are a little LIAR.'

'And Y-Y-YOU,' said Toothless calmly, 'are a r-r-rabbit-hearted, s-s-seaweed-brained, w-w-winkle-eating SNOB.'

Fireworm went for him.

Toothless streaked off, as quick as lightning, and Fireworm's massive jaws snapped together with a sickening crunch on nothing but thin air.

Chaos ensued.

Fireworm completely lost control. She plunged wildly through the air, claws out, biting anything that moved, and letting out great bursts of flame.

Unfortunately, in the process she accidentally scratched Killer, a dragon with a very short temper. Killer then attacked any Hooligan dragon within biting distance.

Soon the dragons were involved in a full-scale, rip-roaring dragonfight, with the boys running around shouting at them to stop and trying to pull them apart without getting killed themselves. The dragons took absolutely no notice whatsoever, however hard the boys yelled – and Thuggory and Snotlout were very red in the face after some pretty impressive yelling.

Gobber the Belch went ballistic on the sidelines. 'CANSOMEBODYTELLMEWHATINTHORAND WODEN'SNAMEISHAPPENING?'

Toothless was in his element in this kind of chaos, dodging Fireworm's angry lunges with ease, nipping in with a lively bite at Alligatiger here and a

DRagonFight ..
Between killer and Fireworm

scratch at Brightclaw there, obviously enjoying the
fight enormously.

Even Horrorcow showed a great deal of spirit
for a dragon who was supposedly vegetarian. She
managed to give Fireworm a truly impressive bite on
the bottom as Fireworm and Killer rolled through the
air biting chunks out of one another.

119

Gobber the Belch entered the fray, grabbing hold of Fireworm's tail. Fireworm gave a howl of outrage, squirmed round, and set Gobber's beard on fire. With one massive hand Gobber swatted out the fire and with the other he clamped Fireworm's jaws together so she could neither bite nor burn. He tucked the furiously enraged animal under one arm, still holding her mouth closed.

'SSSTOPPP!!!!!' screamed Gobber the Belch with a hair-raising, skin-crawling, fang-dropping yell that reverberated off the cliffs, bounced off the sea, and whose faint echoes could be heard on the Mainland.

The boys stopped their useless screaming. The dragons stopped in mid-air.

There was an awful silence.

Even the watching crowd went quiet.

This had never happened before. All twenty boys had shown themselves to be completely out of control of their dragons during the Initiation Test.

Technically, this meant that all of them should be thrown out of their Tribes into exile. And exile in this horrid climate could mean death. Food was scarce, the sea was dangerous, and there were certain wild Tribes in the Isles who were rumoured to be cannibals...

Gobber the Belch stood, lost for words, his beard still smoking.

When he eventually spoke, his voice was deep with the horror of the situation.

'I will have to speak with the Elders of the Tribes,' was all he said. He dropped Fireworm on the ground. She had come to her senses and now slunk towards Snotlout, her tail between her legs.

The Elders of the Tribes were Mogadon and Stoick, Gobber himself, and a few more of the more fearsome warriors, such as Terrible Tuffnut, the Vicious Twins and the Hairy Scary Librarian from the Meathead Public Library. The crowd and the boys stood absolutely still as the Elders consulted in the traditional Elder Huddle, which looked a bit like a rugby scrum.

Meanwhile, the storm was getting worse. Huge claps of thunder burst over their heads, the rain poured down and they couldn't have been much wetter if they had all jumped into the sea.

The Elders consulted for a long time. Mogadon got angry at one point and swung a fist at Tuffnut. A

Twin held on to each of his arms until he calmed down again. Eventually Stoick came out of the Huddle and stood before the boys, who were hanging their heads in shame, their dragons at their feet.

If Hiccup had been able to look at his father, he would have seen that Stoick was not his normal, merry, violent self. He looked very solemn indeed.

'Novices of the Tribes,' he bellowed grimly, 'this is a very bad day for all of you. You have FAILED the Final Test of the Initiation Programme. By the fierce Law of the Inner Isles this means that you should be cast out from the Tribes into exile FOR EVER. I do not want to do this, not only because my own son is among you, but also because it will mean that a whole generation of warriors is lost to the Tribes. But we cannot ignore our Law. Only the strong can belong,

Consulting in the Traditional Elder Huddle

in case the blood of the Tribes should be weakened. Only Heroes can be Hooligans and Meatheads.'

Stoick jabbed a fat finger at the heavens. 'Furthermore,' he carried on, 'the god Thor is really very angry. This is not the moment to weaken our Laws.'

Thor let out a great crash of thunder as if to underline this point.

'Under normal circumstances,' said Stoick, 'the ceremony of exile would start now. But going to sea in weather like this would mean certain death for all concerned. As an act of mercy, I will allow you one more night of shelter under my roof, and first thing tomorrow morning you will be set ashore on the Mainland to fend for yourselves. From this moment forth, you are all banished and may not talk to any other member of your Tribe.'

The thunder crashed all around the boys as they stood, heads bowed, in the rain.

'Pity me, for this is the saddest thing I have ever had to do, to banish my own son,' said Stoick sadly.

The crowd murmured sympathetically, applauding the nobility of their Leader.

'A Chief cannot live like other people,' said

Stoick, looking almost pleadingly at Hiccup. 'He has to decide what is for the good of the Tribe.'

Suddenly Hiccup was very angry.

'Well, don't expect **ME** to pity you!' said Hiccup. 'What kind of father thinks his stupid Laws are more important than his own son? And what kind of stupid Tribe is this anyway, that it can't just have ordinary people in it?'

Stoick stood looking down at his son in surprise and shock for a moment. Then he turned round and trudged off. The Tribes were already running off the beach and scrambling up the hillsides towards the shelter of the Village, lightning coming down all around them.

'I'm going to kill you,' hissed Snotlout at Hiccup, Fireworm snarling menacingly from his shoulder. 'First thing after we're banished, I'm going to kill you,' and he ran off after the others.

'I've lost my t-t-tooth,' Toothless complained whinily. 'C-c-came out when I bit that F-f-fireworm dragon.'

Hiccup took no notice. He looked up at the heavens, beside himself with fury as the wind scooped up sea-water in handfuls and flung it straight into his face.

'JUST ONCE,' yelled Hiccup. 'Why couldn't you let me be a Hero JUST ONCE? I didn't want anything amazing, just to pass this STUPID TEST so I could become a proper Viking like everybody else.'

Thor's thunder boomed and crackled above him blackly.

'OK, THEN,' screamed Hiccup, 'HIT ME with your stupid lightning. Just do something to show you're thinking about me AT ALL.'

But there were to be no bolts of lightning for Hiccup. Thor clearly didn't think he was important enough for an answer. The storm moved on out to sea.

11. THOR IS ANGRY

The storm raged through the whole of that night. Hiccup lay unable to sleep as the wind hurled about the walls like fifty dragons trying to get in.

'Let us in, let us in,' shrieked the wind. 'We're very, very hungry.'

Out in the blackness and way out to sea the storm was so wild and the waves so gigantic that they disturbed the sleep of a couple of very ancient Sea Dragons indeed.

The first Dragon was averagely enormous, about the size of a largeish cliff.

The second Dragon was gobsmackingly vast.

He was that Monster mentioned earlier in this story, the great Beast who had been sleeping off his Roman picnic for the past six centuries or so, the one who had recently been drifting into a lighter sleep.

The great storm lifted both Dragons gently from the seabed like a couple of sleeping babies, and washed them on the swell of one indescribably enormous wave on to The Long Beach, outside Hiccup's village.

And there they stayed, sleeping peacefully, while the wind shrieked horribly all around them like wild Viking ghosts having a loud party in Valhalla, until the storm blew itself out and the sun came up on a beach full of Dragon and very little else.

♥ ♥ ♥

The first Dragon was enough to give you nightmares.

The second Dragon was enough to give your nightmares nightmares.

Imagine an animal about twenty times as large as a Tyrannosaurus Rex. More like a mountain than a living creature – a great, glistening, evil mountain. He was so encrusted with barnacles he looked like he was wearing a kind of jewelled armour but, where the little crustaceans and the coral couldn't get a grip, in the joints and crannies of him, you could see his true colour. A glorious, dark green, it was the colour of the ocean itself.

He was awake now, and he had coughed up the last thing he had eaten, the Standard of the Eighth Legion, with its pathetic ribbons still flying bravely. He was using it as a tooth-pick and the eagle was proving very useful for teasing out those irritating little pieces of flesh that get stuck between your twenty-foot back teeth.

♦ ♦ ♦

The first person to discover the Dragons was Badbreath the Gruff, who set out very early to check how his nets had fared in the storm.

He took one look at the beach, rushed to the Chief's house, and woke him up.

'We have a problem,' said Badbreath.

'What do you mean, **A PROBLEM?**' snapped Stoick the Vast.

Stoick had not slept at all. He had lain awake worrying. What kind of father *did* put his precious Laws before the life of his son? But then what kind of son would fail the precious Laws that his father had looked up to and believed in all his life?

By morning Stoick had made the awesome decision that he was going to reverse the solemn pronouncement he had made on the beach, and un-banish Hiccup and the other boys. 'It is WEAK of me, WEAK,' said Stoick to himself, gloomily. 'Squidface the Terrible would have banished his son in the twinkling of an eye. Loudmouth the Gouty would have positively enjoyed it. What is the *matter* with me? I should be banished myself, and no doubt that is what Mogadon the Meathead is going to suggest.'

All in all, Stoick was not in a state to deal with any more problems.

'There are a couple of humungous Dragons on the Long Beach,' said Badbreath.

'Tell them to go away,' said Stoick.

'*You* tell them,' said Badbreath.

Stoick stomped off to the beach. He returned again looking very thoughtful.

'Did you tell them?' asked Badbreath.

'Tell IT,' said Stoick. 'The larger Dragon has eaten the smaller one. I didn't like to interrupt. I think I shall call a Council of War.'

♥ ♥ ♥

The Hooligans and the Meatheads woke that morning to the terrible sound of the Big Drums summoning them to a Council of War, only used in times of dreadful crisis.

Hiccup awoke with a start. He had hardly slept at all. Toothless, who had crept into bed with Hiccup the night before, was nowhere to be seen and the bed was stone cold, so he had obviously been gone for some time.

Hiccup dragged his clothes on hurriedly. They had dried overnight, and were so stiff with salt that it was like putting on a shirt and leggings made out of wood. He wasn't sure what he was meant to do, as this was the morning he was supposed to go into exile. He followed everybody else to the Great Hall. The Meatheads had spent the night there anyway, because it had not been the weather for camping.

On the way he bumped into Fishlegs. He looked as if he had slept as badly as Hiccup. His glasses were on crooked.

'What's happening?' asked Hiccup. Fishlegs shrugged his shoulders.

'Where's Horrorcow?' asked Hiccup. Fishlegs shrugged his shoulders again.

Hiccup looked around at the crowd pushing its way towards the Great Hall and noticed that there was not a domestic dragon to be seen. Normally they were never far from their Masters' heels and shoulders, yapping and snarling and sneering at each other. There was something faintly sinister about their disappearance...

Nobody else had noticed. There was a tremendous babble of excitement, and such a crush of enormous Vikings that not everybody could get in to the Great Hall, and there was a big jumble of barbarians shouting and shoving outside.

Stoick called for silence.

'I have called you here today,' boomed Stoick, 'because we have a problem on our hands. A rather large Dragon is sitting on the Long Beach.'

The crowd was deeply unimpressed. They were hoping for a more important crisis.

Mogadon voiced the general disapproval.

'The Big Drums are only used in times of ghastly deadly peril,' said Mogadon in amazement. 'You have summoned us here at a horribly early hour,' (Mogadon had not slept well, on the stone floor of the Great Hall with only his helmet for a pillow) 'just because of a DRAGON? I do hope you are not losing your grip, Stoick,' he sneered, hoping that he was.

'This is no ordinary Dragon,' said Stoick. 'This

Dragon is HUGE. Enormous. Gobsmackingly vast. I've never seen anything like it. This is more of a mountain than a Dragon.'

Not having *seen* the Dragon-mountain, the Vikings remained unimpressed. They were used to bossing dragons about.

'The Dragon,' said Stoick, 'must of course, be moved. But it is a very big Dragon. What should we do, Old Wrinkly? You're the thinker in the tribe.'

'You flatter me, Stoick,' said Old Wrinkly, who seemed rather amused by the whole thing. 'It's a Seadragonus Giganticus Maximus, and a particularly big one, I'd say. Very cruel, very intelligent, ravenous appetite. But my field is Early Icelandic Poetry, not large reptiles. Professor Yobbish is the Viking expert on the subject of dragons. Perhaps you should consult his book on the subject.'

'Of course!' said Stoick. '*How to Train Your Dragon,* wasn't it? I do believe that Gobber burgled that very book from the Meathead Public Library...' He gave a naughty look at Mogadon the Meathead.

'This is an outrage!' boomed Mogadon 'that book is Meathead property... I demand its instant return or I shall declare war on the spot.'

'Oh, put a sock in it, Mogadon,' said Stoick. 'With soppy librarians like yours, what can you expect?'

The Hairy Scary Librarian blushed a delicate pink and shook in his size eighteen shoes.

'Baggybum, hand me the book from the fireplace,' yelled Stoick.

Baggybum stretched out one of his great octopus arms and picked the book off the shelf. He lobbed it across the heads of the crowd and Stoick caught it, to much cheering. Morale was high. Stoick bowed to the hordes and handed the book to Gobber.

'GOB-BER, GOB-BER, GOB-BER,' yelled the crowd. It was Gobber's moment of triumph. A crisis demands a Hero and he knew he was the man for the job. His chest swelled with self-importance.

'Oh, it was nothing really…' he bellowed modestly, 'a bit of Basic Burglary you know… Keeps me in practice…'

'Sssssssh,' hissed the crowd like sea-snakes, as Gobber cleared his throat.

'How to Train Your Dragon,' announced Gobber solemnly. He paused.

'YELL AT IT.'

There was another pause.

134

'And…?' said Stoick. 'Yell at it, and…?'

'That's it,' said Gobber. 'YELL AT IT.'

'There's nothing in there about the Seadragonus Giganticus Maximus in particular?' asked Stoick.

Gobber looked through the book again. 'Not as such,' said Gobber. 'Just the bit about yelling at it, really.'

'Hmmm,' said Stoick. 'It's brief, isn't it? I've never noticed before, but it is brief… Brief but to the point,' he added hastily, 'like us Vikings. Thank Thor for our experts. Now,' said Stoick, in his most Chief-like manner, 'since it is such a large Dragon—'

'Vast,' interrupted Old Wrinkly happily. 'Gigantic. Stupendously enormous. Five times as big as the Big Blue Whale.'

'Yes, thank you, Old Wrinkly,' said Stoick. 'Since it is, indeed, on the rather large side, we're going to need a rather large yell. I want everybody on the clifftops yelling at the same time.'

'What shall we yell?' asked Baggybum.

'Something brief and to the point. GO AWAY,' said Stoick.

♥ ♥ ♥

The Tribes of Meathead and Hooligan gathered at the

top of the cliffs of The Long Beach and looked down at the impossibly vast Serpent stretched out on the sand, smacking its lips as it devoured the last morsels of its late unfortunate companion. It was so big that it seemed unlikely that it could be alive, until you saw it move like an earthquake or a trick of the eyes.

There are times when size really is *important*, thought Hiccup to himself. *And this is one of them*.

Dragons are vain, cruel and amoral creatures, as I've said. This is all very well when they are a lot smaller than you are. But when a dragon's bad nature is multiplied into something the size of a hillside, how do you deal with it?

Gobber the Belch stepped forward to lead the yelling, as the most respected Yeller among them all. His chest swelled with pride.

'One... two... three...'

Four hundred Viking voices screamed as one: 'GO AWAY!' and added for good measure the Viking War Cry.

The Viking War Cry was designed to chill the blood of Viking enemies at the commencement of battle. It is a horrifying, electrifying shriek that begins by mimicking the furious yell of a swooping predator, which then turns into the victim's scream of pure terror, and ends with a horribly realistic imitation of the death-gurgles as he chokes on his own blood.

It is a scary noise at the best of times, but shouted altogether by four hundred barbarians at eight o'clock in the morning it was enough to make the mighty Thor himself drop his hammer and blub like a little baby.

There was an impressive silence.

The mighty Dragon then turned his mighty head in their direction.

There were four hundred gasps as a pair of evil, yellow eyes, as big as six tall men, narrowed down to slits.

The Dragon opened its mouth and let out a sound so loud and so terrifying that four or five passing seagulls dropped down dead with fear on the spot. It was a noise that made the Viking War Cry seem like the faint cry of a newborn baby in comparison. It was a terrible alien other-worldly noise that promised DEATH and NO MERCY and EVERYTHING AWFUL.

There was another impressive silence.

With one delicate movement of his talon, the

THE DRAGON flicked.
GOBBER THE BELCH as if
he were a spit ball...

Dragon ripped through Gobber's tunic and trousers
from head to toe as if he were peeling fruit. Gobber
gave a most un-Heroic shriek of outraged modesty.
The Dragon placed the same talon upright in front of
Gobber the Belch and flicked him like a spitball,
way, way away, over the Vikings' heads and over the
walled fortifications of the village.

The Dragon put his vast, cracked old paw to
his reptilian lips and blew the Vikings a kiss. The kiss

streaked through the sky and scored a direct hit on both Stoick and Mogadon's ships, which had survived the storm and were rocking in the safety of Hooligan Harbour. All fifty of them burst simultaneously into flames.

The Vikings ran away from that cliff as fast as their eight hundred legs could carry them.

♦ ♦ ♦

Gobber the Belch had the luck to land on the roof of his own house. The deep layers of soggy grass broke his fall as he went through them, and he ended up sitting stark-naked in his own chair in front of the fire, dazed but unharmed.

'OK, then,' said Stoick to four hundred Vikings suddenly looking scared but wildly over-excited, 'so the Yelling doesn't work.'

They had reassembled in the centre of the village.

'And, as our fleet is out of action, we have no means of escape from the island,' Stoick continued. 'What we need now,' he said, trying to sound as if he was on top of the situation, 'is for somebody to go and ask the monster whether he comes in PEACE or in WAR.'

'I shall go…' volunteered Gobber who rejoined them at that moment, still determined to be the Hero of the hour. He was trying to sound noble and dignified but it is very difficult to be truly dignified with grass in your hair and wearing your cousin Agatha's dress – which was the only thing Gobber could find to wear in the house.

'Do you speak Dragonese, Gobber?' asked

GOBBER THE BELCH trying to look tough while dressed in Cousin Agatha's dress..

Stoick in surprise.

'Well, no,' Gobber admitted. 'Nobody here speaks Dragonese. It's forbidden by order of Stoick the Vast, O Hear His Name and Tremble, Ugh, Ugh. Dragons are inferior creatures who we yell at. Dragons might get above themselves if we talk to them. Dragons are tricksy and must be kept in their place.'

'Hiccup can speak to dragons,' said Fishlegs very quietly, from the middle of the crowd.

'Sssh, Fishlegs,' whispered Hiccup, desperately digging his friend in the ribs.

'Well, you can,' said Fishlegs stoutly. 'Don't you see? This is your chance to be a Hero. And we're all going to die anyway, so you might as well take it...'

'Hiccup can speak to dragons!' shouted Fishlegs, very loudly indeed.

'Hiccup?' said Gobber the Belch.

'HICCUP?' said Stoick the Vast.

'Yes, Hiccup,' said Old Wrinkly. 'Small boy, red hair, freckles, you were going to put him into exile this morning.' Old Wrinkly looked stern. 'In order that the blood of the Tribes should not be weakened, remember? Your son, Hiccup.'

'I know who Hiccup *is*, thank you, Old Wrinkly,'

said Stoick the Vast, uncomfortably. 'Does anyone know *where* he is? HICCUP! Come forward.'

'It looks like you could come in useful after all...' Old Wrinkly murmured to himself.

'Here he is!' yelled Fishlegs, patting Hiccup on the back. Hiccup started to wriggle through the crowd until somebody noticed him and dragged him up, and he was passed over everybody's heads and put down in front of Stoick.

'Hiccup,' said Stoick. 'Is it true that you can talk to dragons?'

Hiccup nodded.

Stoick gave an awkward cough. 'This is an embarrassing situation. I know that we were about to banish you from the Tribe. However, if you do what I ask, I am sure I speak for everybody when I say that you can consider yourself un-banished. We stand in awful peril and nobody else in this room can speak Dragonese. Will you go to this monster and ask him whether he comes in PEACE or in WAR?'

Hiccup said nothing.

Stoick coughed again. 'You can talk to me,' said Stoick. 'I've un-banished you.'

'So the exile is off, then, is it, Father?' asked

Hiccup. 'If I go and kill myself talking to this Beast from Hell, I will be considered Heroic enough to join the Tribe of Hooligans?'

Stoick looked more embarrassed than ever. 'Absolutely,' he said.

'OK, then,' said Hiccup. 'I'll do it.'

Hiccup looking determined

12. THE GREEN DEATH

It is one thing to approach a primeval nightmare when you are part of a crowd of four hundred people. It is quite another to do so on your own. Hiccup had to force himself to put one foot in front of the other.

Stoick offered to send a guard of his finest soldiers, but Hiccup preferred to go alone. 'Less chance of anybody doing anything Heroic and stupid,' he said.

Although this is the part of the story that the bards tend to focus on as the bit where Hiccup was particularly Heroic, I do not agree. It is a lot easier to be brave when you know you have no alternative. Hiccup knew in his heart of hearts that the Monster intended to kill them all anyway. So he didn't have a lot to lose.

Nonetheless, he was sweating as he peered over the edge of the cliff. There, below him, was the impossibly large Dragon, filling up the beach. It appeared to be asleep.

But an eerie singing was coming from the direction of its belly. The song went something like this:

'Watch me, Great Destroyer,
    as I settle down to lunch,
Killer whales are tasty 'cos they've
    got a lot of crunch.
Great white sharks are scrumptious,
    but here's a little tip:
Those teeny weeny pointy teeth can
    give a nasty nip...'

How odd, thought Hiccup, *he can sing with his mouth shut*.

Hiccup nearly jumped clear out of his leggings when the Dragon opened both his crocodile eyes and spoke directly to him

'Why so odd?' said the Dragon, who appeared to be amused. 'A dragon with his eyes shut is not necessarily asleep, so it follows that a dragon with his mouth shut is not necessarily singing. All is not what it seems. That noise that you hear is not me at all. THAT, my Hero, is the sound of a singing supper.'

'A singing supper?' echoed Hiccup, quickly remembering that you should never, ever, look into the eyes of a large, malevolent Dragon like this one.

He fixed his gaze firmly on
one of the Dragon's talons instead.

This was a mistake, as Hiccup suddenly realised
that the Dragon was holding a herd of pathetically
bleating sheep captive under one massive claw. He
pretended to allow one of them to escape, let the
poor animal practically reach the safety of the rocks,
then picked it up by its wool with a delicate pincer
movement and tossed it way, way up into the air.

This was a trick Hiccup had often done himself,
but with blackberries. Now the Dragon threw back
his great head and the woolly speck fell down into the
terrible jaws, which closed behind it with a mighty
crash. There was a horrible sound of crunching as he
chewed and swallowed the unfortunate sheep.

The Dragon saw Hiccup watching him in
fascinated horror and he brought his ridiculously
enormous head down closer to the boy. Hiccup nearly

passed out as his offensive Dragon-breath poured out
in a disgusting, yellow-green vapour. It was the stench
of DEATH itself – a deep, head-spinning stench of
decaying matter; of rotting haddock heads and
sweating whale; of long-dead shark and despairing
souls. The revolting steam curled its way around the
boy in repellent coils and wormed its way up into his
nose until he coughed and spluttered.

'Some people say you should de-bone a sheep
before you eat it,' sneered the Dragon confidentially,
'but I think it adds just a nice crunch to what would
otherwise be a bit of a soggy meal...'

The Dragon burped. The belch came out as a
perfect loop of fire that soared through the air like
a smoke ring and landed on the heather surrounding
Hiccup, setting it alight, so that for a moment he was
standing right in the middle of a circle of bright green
flames. The heather was damp, however, and the blaze
flared for only a few moments, then extinguished
itself.

'Ooops,' giggled the Dragon evilly. 'Pardon me...
A little party trick...'

He then placed one gigantic claw against the
edge of the cliff that Hiccup was standing on.

148

'Humans, however,' continued the Dragon thoughtfully, 'humans really *should* be filleted. The spine in particular can be very tickly as it goes down the throat...'

As the Dragon spoke, he extended his claws, the talons slowly emerging from the thick stumps of his fingers and rising up until they resembled nothing more than gigantic razors, six feet wide and twenty feet long, with points on the end like a surgeon's scalpel.

'Removing the human backbone is a delicate job,' hissed the Dragon nastily, 'but one that I am particularly good at... a small incision at the back of the neck' – he gestured at Hiccup's neck – 'a swift stroke downwards, then flick it out... it's practically painless. For ME...'

The Dragon's eyes lit up with the purest pleasure.

Hiccup was thinking very fast indeed. There is nothing like staring Death in the face for speeding up your thoughts. What did he know about dragons that could work against an Invincible Monster like this one?

He could see the Dragon Motivation page he had written in his mind's eye. GRATITUDE: dragons are *never* grateful. FEAR: clearly hopeless. GREED: not a good idea to appeal to at this particular point in time. VANITY and REVENGE: could be useful but he couldn't quite think how. That left JOKES AND RIDDLING TALK. This Dragon looked a bit exalted for jokes. But from his manner of talking he clearly fancied himself as a bit of a philosopher. Maybe Hiccup could buy himself some time if he engaged him in a riddling conversation…

'I've heard of singing *for* your supper,' said Hiccup, 'but what is *a* singing supper?'

'A good question,' said the Dragon, in surprise. 'An EXCELLENT question, in fact.' He drew back his claws and Hiccup sighed with relief. 'It's a long time since the supper has shown such intelligence. They're generally too bound up with their titchy little lives to bother with the Really Big Questions.

'Now let me think,' said the Dragon and, as he thought, he forked a protesting sheep on the end of a talon, then chewed on it reflectively. Hiccup was sorry for the sheep but deeply grateful that it wasn't *him* disappearing down the ravenous reptilian gullet.

'How shall I put it, to a brain *so much* smaller and less clever than mine... The thing is, we are all, in a sense, supper. Walking, talking, breathing suppers, that's what we are. Take you, for instance. YOU are about to be eaten by ME, so that makes *you* supper. That's obvious. But even a murderous carnivore like myself will be a supper for worms one day. We're all snatching precious moments from the peaceful jaws of time,' said the Dragon cheerfully.

'That's why it's so important,' he continued, 'for the supper to sing as beautifully as it can.'

He gestured to his stomach, from where the voice could still be heard singing, though more and more faintly.

> *'Humans can be bland,*
> > *but if you have some salt to hand,*
> *A little bit of brine,*
> > *will make them taste divi-I-I-ne...'*

151

'That PARTICULAR supper,' said the Dragon, 'that you hear singing now, was a dragon rather smaller than me, but very full of himself. I ate him about half an hour ago.'

'Isn't that cannibalism?' asked Hiccup.

'It's delicious,' said the Dragon. 'Besides, you can't call an ARTIST like myself a CANNIBAL.' He sounded a bit exasperated now. 'You are very rude for such a small person. What do you want, Little Supper?'

'I have come,' said Hiccup, 'to find out whether you come in PEACE or in WAR.'

'Oh, peace, I think,' said the Dragon. 'I *am* going to kill you though,' he added.

'*All* of us?' asked Hiccup.

'You first,' said the Dragon kindly. 'And then everybody else when I've had a little nap and got my appetite back. It takes a little while to wake up completely from a Sleep Coma.'

'But it's all so unfair!' said Hiccup. 'Why do YOU get to eat everybody, just because you're bigger than everybody else?'

'It's the way of the world,' said the Dragon. 'Besides, you'll find that you come round to my point-of-view once you're inside me. That's the marvellous thing about digestion... But where are my manners? Let me introduce myself. I am the Green Death. What is your name, Little Supper?'

'Hiccup Horrendous Haddock the Third,' said Hiccup.

And the most extraordinary thing happened.

As Hiccup said his name the Green Death trembled, as if a sudden wind had made him shiver. Neither the Green Death nor Hiccup noticed.

'Hmmm...' said the Green Death. 'I'm sure I've heard that name somewhere before. But it's rather a mouthful so I shall just call you Little Supper. Now, Little Supper, before I eat you, tell me your problem.'

'My problem?' asked Hiccup.

'That's right,' said the Dragon. 'Your Why-Can't-I-Be-More-Like-My-Father? problem. Your It's-Hard-to-Be-a-Hero problem. Your Snotlout-Would-Make-a-Better-Chief-Than-Me problem. I have helped the problems of many a Supper. Somehow meeting a Really Big Problem like myself seems to put everything else in proportion.'

'Let me get this straight,' said Hiccup. 'You

know all about my father, and me not being a Hero and everything –'

'I can see things like that,' said the Green Death modestly.

'– and you want me to tell you my problems and then you're going to eat me?'

'We're back at the beginning again,' sighed the Green Death. 'We're *all* going to be eaten SOMETIME. You can win yourself some extra time, though, if you're a smart little crabstick. A few scraps from the burning...'

The Green Death yawned.

'I'm suddenly rather tired,' he said. 'You ARE a clever little crabstick, you've kept me talking for AGES...' and the Dragon yawned again. 'I'm too tired to eat you right now, you'll have to come back in a couple of hours... and I'll tell you how to deal with your problem then. I have a feeling I can help you...'

And the terrible monster really *did* fall asleep this time, and snored most heavily. His great claws relaxed and fell open and the remaining sheep, their woolly sides trembling with terror, scrambled over the tops of the terrible talons and bolted up the cliff path.

Hiccup stood watching the Dragon thoughtfully

for a second, then he trudged slowly back through the heather towards the village.

Everybody cheered when he walked through the gates. He was carried shoulder high and set down in front of his father.

'Well, son,' said Stoick. 'Does the beast come in **PEACE** or in **WAR**?'

'He says he comes in peace,' said Hiccup. There were huge hurrahs and heavy stampings of feet.

Hiccup held up his hand for silence.

'He's still going to kill us, though.'

... A-a-a-argh ...

13. WHEN YELLING DOESN'T WORK

The Dragon slept on as the Council of War argued about what to do next.

'I am going to write a strongly-worded letter to Professor Yobbish,' said Stoick the Vast. 'This book needs a lot more WORDS to tell you what to do if yelling doesn't work.'

Which shows how cross Stoick was – he never wrote a letter if he could help it.

Stoick, in fact, was really rattled, for the first time in his life.

This is what comes of not following the Law, he thought to himself. *If I had banished the boys last night like I should have done, they would not be here to die with the rest of us. I should have put my trust in Thor.*

Mogadon the Meathead had not yet realised the gravity of the situation. He thought it was a question of constructing some sort of megaphone machine to make the Yell sound bigger.

'A gigantic dragon just needs a gigantic Yell,'

he said.

'We already TRIED that, O Plankton Brain,' said Stoick.

'WHO ARE YOU CALLING PLANKTON BRAIN?' demanded Mogadon and they went whisker to whisker like a couple of furious walruses.

Hiccup sighed and walked out of the village.

He had a feeling the grown-ups weren't going to come up with anything fiendishly clever.

To Hiccup's surprise he was followed, not only by Fishlegs but by all the Novices from both the Hooligan AND the Meathead tribes.

They stood around Hiccup in a semi-circle.

'So, Hiccup,' said Thuggory the Meathead. 'What are we going to do now, then?'

'Whaddyamean by asking HICCUP?' demanded Snotlout crossly. 'You're not going to ask THE USELESS to get us out of this mess, are you? He just single-handedly got us all to fail the Final Initiation Test. We were about to be banished and eaten by cannibals all because of HIM. He can't even control a dragon the size of an earwig!'

'Can YOU talk to dragons then, Snotface?' asked Fishlegs.

'I am pleased to say I cannot,' said Snotlout, with dignity.

'Well, shut up, then,' said Fishlegs.

Snotlout got hold of Fishlegs by the arm and started twisting.

'Nobody, but NOBODY, tells SNOTFACE SNOTLOUT to shut up,' hissed Snotlout.

'*I* do,' said Thuggory the Meathead. He grabbed Snotlout by the shirt and lifted him clear off the ground. 'YOUR dragon got us failed just as much as HIS. I didn't notice *anybody's* dragon sitting up and begging like a good boy in the middle of that dragon-fight. YOU shut up or I will tear you limb from limb and feed you to the gulls, you winkle-hearted, seaweed-brained, limpet-eating PIG.'

Snotlout looked into Thuggory's stern little eyes.

Snotlout shut up.

Thuggory dropped him and wiped his hands disdainfully on his tunic. 'Anyway,' said Thuggory, 'MY father was on that stupid Council of Elders too. I'm with Hiccup. What kind of father puts his stupid Laws before the life of his son? And what kind of stupid Test was that, anyway? If we save all those stupid people from a REAL dragon like this one, maybe

158

YOU shut up or I will tear you limb from limb and feed you to the gulls, you winkle-hearted, seaweed-brained, limpet eating PIG.

they'll let us into their stupid Tribe after all.'

WELL, WELL, WELL, thought Hiccup. *This is a turn up for the books. Maybe that Dragon was right and he is going to help me with my It's-Hard-to-Be-a-Hero problem. Before he eats me, of course.*

One solo meeting with the Green Death and here were nineteen young barbarians, most of them much bigger and tougher and rougher than Hiccup, looking at Hiccup expectantly to tell them what to do.

Hiccup stood on tiptoe and tried to look like a Hero.

'OK,' said Hiccup. 'I need some time to think.'

'**GIVE THE BOY SOME ROOM HERE!**' yelled Thuggory, pushing all the others back.

He swept off a rock for Hiccup to sit on.

'You just do all the thinking you need, boyo,' said Thuggory. 'This is a situation that needs a lot of thought and I have a feeling you're the only one here who can do it. Anybody who can have a twenty minute conversation with a winged shark the size of a planet and come out of it alive is a better thinker than I am.'

Hiccup found himself warming to Thuggory the Meathead.

'QUIET!' yelled Thuggory. 'HICCUP IS THINKING.'

Hiccup thought.

And thought.

♦ ♦ ♦

After about half an hour, Thuggory said: 'Whatever you're thinking about to get rid of that monster better work for both of them.'

'There's ANOTHER Dragon?' asked Hiccup.

Thuggory nodded.

'I went up to the Highest Point and spotted him while you were having your chat with the Big Green One.'

'OK,' said Hiccup. 'That's good news, actually. Let's check out the new Horror.'

The trail up to the Highest Point was littered with scallop shells and dolphin's bones thrown up by the gigantic storm. Along the way they even passed the wreck of one of Stoick's favourite ships, *The Pure Adventure*, lost at sea seven years before, and now perched crazily on a rock three quarters of the way up the biggest hill on Berk.

Once you were right at the top it was possible to see most of Berk's coastline and the sea encircling you on all sides. Right at the other end of the island, a Dragon entirely filled up Unlandable Cove and spilled over the sides.

He was resting his vast, wicked chin on the cliff as a pillow. Great plumes of violet smoke were belching out of his snoring nostrils.

He was another Seadragonus Giganticus Maximus, this time a glorious deep purple in colour and, if anything, slightly larger than the one at Long Beach.

'The Purple Death, I presume,' whispered Hiccup, shakily. 'This is just what we need. Are you sure there aren't any more?'

Thuggory laughed, slightly hysterically. 'I think it's just the two nightmare killing-machines. Two not enough for you?'

♥ ♥ ♥

Back at the Highest Point, Hiccup outlined his Plan of Action.

It was Fiendishly Clever – if a bit desperate.

'We aren't big enough to fight these dragons,' said Hiccup, 'but they *can* fight EACH OTHER. We have to get them *really* angry at one another. We Hooligans will concentrate on the Green Death and

162

you Meatheads will deal with the Purple Death.

'The one thing we will need is our own dragons, who seem to have disappeared,' said Hiccup, 'so we'd better start calling for them.'

They started calling for their dragons, as loudly as they dared, and then louder still as there was no response.

The twenty dragons that belonged to the Novices were not, in fact, very far away at all. They had made up after the dragon-fight and were now hiding in a piece of boggy bracken about a hundred yards or so away from where the boys were standing on the Highest Point. They were crouching like giant cats in the ferns, wicked eyes gleaming. They were now so exactly the shade of a clump of bracken that they seemed to have melted entirely into the bog. If you had been a rabbit or a deer you would not have noticed them

Newtsbreath

163

until you felt the talons on your back and the hot fire on your neck.

They had been following the boys for a while.

'So,' whispered Fireworm, her tongue flickering menacingly. 'What do we do now then? The power is shifting on this island. The Masters will not be Masters for much longer. They are trapped, like lobsters in a pot. We are not. We can fly whenever we want. Do we obey or do we desert?'

Dragons are not the sort of creatures to back a loser.

'Whatever we do,' grumbled Brightclaw, 'let's do it QUICKLY, my wings are freezing up.'

Brightclaw

'We could kill the boys now and take them as an offering to the New Master,' suggested Seaslug, with a grunt of greedy pleasure.

'What, that great green Devil on the beach?' said Horrorcow placidly. 'I don't like the look of him, myself. He has too big an appetite. We might find ourselves as the next offering.'

'We fly, then,' said Brightclaw, and the others murmured their agreement.

'S-s-silence,' hissed Fireworm. 'These islands are perilous,' she sneered. 'We might fly from one danger straight into the mouth of another. I say we obey, until we are *sure* that they have lost. When that time comes I will give the signal for us to desert.'

And so, as if from nowhere, Fireworm and Seaslug, Horrorcow and Killer, Brightclaw and Alligatiger and all the other dragons flew out of their hiding-place and came circling slowly up to the Highest Point, landing on each boy's outstretched arm.

Last of all came Toothless, complaining horribly.

'Dragons...' said Hiccup.

And he explained the Fiendishly Clever Plan.

14. THE FIENDISHLY CLEVER PLAN

The dragons protested a bit, but the boys yelled them into line.

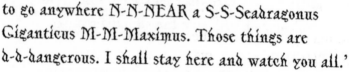

All except for Toothless, who absolutely refused to join in.

'Y-y-you must be j-j-joking,' sneered the little dragon. 'I refuse to go anywhere N-N-NEAR a S-S-Seadragonus Giganticus M-M-Maximus. Those things are d-d-dangerous. I shall stay here and watch you all.'

Hiccup coaxed and bribed and threatened in vain.

'You see?' said Snotlout. 'The Useless can't even get his *own* dragon to carry out his pathetic plan. And THIS is the person you are banking on to get you out of this mess?'

'Ugh,' said Dogsbreath the Duhbrain.

'Oh, SHUDDUP, Snotlout,' chorused the rest of the boys.

Hiccup sighed and gave up. 'OK then,

Toothless, you just stay here and miss all the fun. Now, I want everybody to go down to the Gull's Nesting Place and collect as many birds' feathers as you can for the feather bombs—'

'Birds' feathers!' scoffed Snotlout. 'This wimp thinks you can fight an animal like THAT with birds' feathers! Cold steel is the only language a creature like that will understand.'

'Dragons have a tendency to asthma,' explained Hiccup. 'It's all that fire-breathing they do. The smoke gets in their lungs.'

'So you think this monster is going to die from asthma right then and there because of a few FEATHER BOMBS? Why not just feed him fried herring and see whether he drops dead of a heart attack in twenty years or so?' jeered Snotlout.

'No,' said Hiccup patiently, 'the feather bombs are just to make him very confused so he won't kill anybody on the way. Snotlout, Thuggory, I'm going to need to coach Fireworm and Killer in what they have to say,' continued Hiccup.

'I'm not putting *my* dragon at risk in this crazy plan,' said Snotlout.

'OH YES, YOU ARE,' hissed Thuggory,

through gritted teeth, brandishing a massive fist at
Snotlout.

'This guy is such a PAIN, Hiccup, I don't know
how you put up with him. Listen, Snotfeatures, by
some miracle you have got yourself a reasonable
dragon. You GET that dragon to do what Hiccup
wants or it will give me much pleasure to
PERSONALLY boot you all the way to Porpoise
Point and back again.'

'OK, then,' said Snotlout crossly. 'But don't
blame me when we all get barbecued because of the
Useless's mad idea.'

♦ ♦ ♦

Hiccup supervised the making of the feather bombs.

The boys gathered great armfuls of feathers
from the Gull's Nesting Place.

They then burgled every item of material they
could find: Goggletoad's nappies, Gobber's pyjamas,
Mogadon the Meathead's tent, Vallhallarama's bra –
anything they could get their hands on. The grown-ups
were too busy consulting amongst themselves to take
any notice.

Snotlout cheered up a bit because he could show
off his superior skill at Burglary. He managed to steal

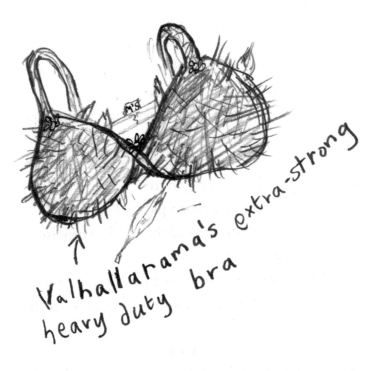

Valhallarama's extra-strong
heavy duty bra

BAGGYBUM'S
hairy
KNICKERS

Baggybum the Beerbelly

Baggybum's knickers right off him as he was standing in a Huddle discussing a Plan of Action. Baggybum didn't notice, not even when he reached a hairy hand down to absentmindedly scratch his great bottom – he was too busy talking about Bigger and Better Methods of Yelling.

The boys then wrapped the feathers up in the material, so that they would fly out when the bomb was dropped.

Each team of ten boys was armed with about a hundred of these feather bombs, wrapped in a great parcel made out of an old sail.

Hiccup led the Hooligans towards The Long Beach, while Thuggory took the Meatheads to Unlandable Cove.

The thin column of boys were excitedly chattering as they set off behind Hiccup; Wartihog and Clueless dragging the sail at the rear, the dragons circling and diving a couple of feet above their heads. Vikings are practically fearless, having been bred to be soldiers, so even Hiccup and Fishlegs had a surge of excitement at the thought of the battle to come.

But as soon as the monster came into sight again, the boys and the dragons instantly dropped to their tummies and squirmed forward, hearts beating hard.

It was impossible that ANYTHING could be THAT big.

Hiccup led them as near as he dared to the edge of the cliffs surrounding The Long Beach.

They looked down on the terrible creature snoring in front of them. His nostrils alone were as big as six front doors, and the stench reeking out of them made it difficult for the boys to breathe.

Wartihog, who had always had a delicate stomach, threw up disgustingly in the heather.

Hiccup, Fishlegs and Clueless unwrapped the feather bombs and gave one to each boy. The boys called the dragons, as softly as they could, and each put a feather bomb in their dragon's mouth.

They then stood up on the edge of the cliff with their dragons on their outstretched arms.

This took about the same amount of bravery it might take for you to leap off a mountain at a thousand feet. Even with the monster fast asleep, the natural reaction was to keep hidden in the bracken.

Hiccup tried not to breathe in.

He lifted his arm to give the command to begin.

'Go,' whispered Hiccup.

'GO!' yelled back the boys, and ten dragons flew up and circled around the vast sleeping head.

Just as the Green Death inhaled, Hiccup shouted 'NOW!' and the dragons let go of the feather bombs.

The Green Death took in a breath that was half air and half feathers. He woke with a gigantic sneeze and, as he shuddered and coughed, Fireworm, who was treading air near his right ear, gave a speech which went something like this, but a lot more irritating:

'Greetings, O Seadragonus Pusillanimus Minimus, from my Father, the Terror of the Seas. He is feeling like feasting on the barbarians and if you get in his way he will feast on YOU. Swim away, little seaslug, and you will be safe – but stay on this island and you will feel the sharpness of his claws and the fierceness of his fire.'

Fireworm leads the way in
Operation Sneeze Attack.
Ilhallarama's bra makes a particularly
effective double bomb...

The Giant Monster tried to laugh sarcastically and cough at the same time, but this is virtually impossible, and a feather went down the wrong way, making him cough even more.

Then Fireworm bit him on the nose.

It must have felt like a flea bite but the Monster was outraged.

Through streaming eyes, the Green Death made a swipe at this irritating dragon-flea and missed. One giant claw tore down part of the cliff-face instead.

The nine other dragons had by this time returned to collect more feather bombs from the boys on the cliffs.

'NOW!' yelled Hiccup and, with split-second timing, they let their bombs fly. They hit their target of the Green Death's nostrils and he collapsed with coughing again.

'You cannot win, puny worm,' crowed Fireworm. 'Wriggle back to the sea where you belong and let my Master have his supper.'

Now the Green Death was *really* cross.

He bounded lopsidedly after Fireworm, trying to bat away this irritating little speck of a dragon with his claws.

But the Green Death had the same sort of difficulty in catching Fireworm as you might have if you tried to catch a bluebottle with your bare hands. Dragons are better than humans at that sort of game but the Green Death kept on missing because his eyes were streaming so much.

'Missed again!' sneered Fireworm, enjoying herself hugely – and she flapped just out of reach of the Green Death's claws. The Green Death made another wild leap towards her, as Fireworm flew on around the corner of the cliffs, steering the monster in the direction of Unlandable Cove.

Hiccup and the boys ran after them as fast as they could, but they hadn't a hope of keeping up. Running through heather is not unlike running through knee-deep treacle, and they kept disappearing up to their knees in the bog.

As Fireworm and the Monster got further and further ahead in their race along the shore line, it took longer and longer for the other dragons to fly back to the boys and return with more feather bombs.

The military commanders among you will recognize the kind of problems that ensue when the supply line can no longer reach the forces at the front.

Eventually it was taking so long to reload that there came a moment when there were no more feathers tickling the Green Death's nostrils and his eyes stopped streaming and suddenly he could see the maddening Fireworm pinpoint clear…

The Green Death made a lightning reflex swipe at the red dragon and caught her in one gigantic claw.

It was lucky for Fireworm that at that very moment the Purple Death came crashing round the corner and struck the Green Death heavily in the stomach. His grip loosened on Fireworm for a second and she flew off, panting with relief.

The Green Death sat down heavily in the sea and fought for breath.

The Purple Death did much the same.

15. THE BATTLE AT DEATH'S HEAD HEADLAND

While Hiccup and his team had been enraging the Green Death, Thuggory and *his* team had been infuriating the Purple Death.

The two monsters ran smack into one another as they met at the corner of Death's Head Headland.

One of Fireworm's wings was broken in two places from her experience in the Green Death's grip but she bravely flew back and made her final speech into his ear, as he sat gasping for air in the shallows.

'Here he is,' shouted Fireworm. 'My Master, the Purple Horror, who will tear you limb from limb and spit out your toenails!'

And Fireworm flew away lopsidedly as fast as she could, with one wing trailing behind her.

♦ ♦ ♦

The Green Death was having a bad day.

Ordinarily, a Seadragonus Giganticus Maximus would not dream of attacking another animal of the same breed. They avoid fighting each other because they know they are so heavily armed that the battle risks ending in death for both of them.

However, the Green Death had been attacked and jeered at by minuscule creatures who had inflamed and outraged his vanity. This Creature, who seemed to think he was tougher than the Green Death himself, had struck him heavily in the chest.

The Green Death wasn't thinking too hard.

He leapt at the Purple Death with his talons outstretched, breathing great bursts of fire, which lit up the landscape all around like lightning.

The ground and the sea shook in great earthquakes as the two gigantic monsters lunged crazily at each other, swearing the most unrepeatable oaths in Dragonese.

The Green Death's foot completely destroyed Wrecker's Reef with one blow.

The Purple Death's wings caused great landslides to come tumbling down from the Headland's cliffs.

Now their job was done, the Viking boys were running away as fast as they could, their eyes popping with terror, in case one of the dragons survived the fight. Every now and then they looked back to see how the battle was going.

With ghastly, eerie cries, the Dragons slashed and bit and tore pieces off one another.

The Sea Dragon is the most well-defended creature that has ever lived on this planet. Its skin is over three feet thick in places, and so encrusted with shells and barnacles that it almost has the effect of armour.

It is also the most well-armed creature that has ever lived on this planet and its razor sharp claws and teeth can rip open its own iron crust as if it were made out of paper…

Now both Dragons had terrible wounds, and their green lifeblood was pouring out of them.

The Green Death gripped the Purple Death around the neck with a deadly Throatchoker Grip.

The Purple Death hugged the Green Death around the chest with a deadly Breathquencher Hug.

Neither would let go – and the grip of a Dragon is a terrible thing. They reminded Hiccup of a picture on one of his father's shields: of two dragons forming a perfect circle as they ate one another, each with a tail in their mouth.

The Dragons thrashed around wildly in the surf,

179

gagging and choking, with their eyes popping, their tails causing such tidal waves that the boys were soaked, even though they were scrambling away from the Headland as fast as they could.

Finally, with some last heaving shudders and grim gurgles, both mighty beasts lay still in the water.

There was silence.

The boys stopped running. They stood gasping for breath, watching the motionless beasts with dread. The boys' dragons, which were flying some way ahead of the boys, also turned, and hung still in the air.

The Terrible Creatures didn't move.

The boys waited two long minutes, as waves lapped gently over the great, motionless bodies.

'They're dead,' said Thuggory at last.

The boys started laughing, rather hysterically, now that the terror was over.

'Well done, Hiccup!' Thuggory slapped Hiccup on the back.

But Hiccup was looking worried. He was squinting his eyes and straining to hear something. 'I can't hear anything,' said Hiccup anxiously.

'You can't hear anything because they're DEAD,' said Thuggory joyfully. 'Three cheers for Hiccup!'

Halfway through the boys' cheering, Fireworm let out a terrible noise. 'DESERT!' she shrieked. 'Desert, desert, desert, desert!'

The head of the corpse of the Green Death was slowly lifting up and turning in their direction.

'Uh-oh,' said Hiccup.

'uh-oh...'

16. THE FIENDISHLY CLEVER PLAN GOES WRONG

Hiccup had been listening for the Green Death's Death Song, but he wasn't singing it yet.

The Green Death was dying, but he wasn't dead yet.

What he *was* was very, very angry indeed.

Out of his bleeding mouth he hissed weakly, *'Where is he?'*

And then he heaved himself on to his feet, and hissed a little more strongly, 'WHERE is he? Where IS the Little Supper? I knew I recognised him, he was my doom, no wonder. The Little Supper has made a Supper of ME, the Green Death himself!'

As the Dragon spoke, he was inching forwards very slowly and painfully, his eyes fixed on the cliff top, where he could see little human beings beginning to run inland again.

The Dragon threw back his head and SCREAMED a blood-chilling scream of pure horrid REVENGE, dark and torturous.

'I'LL supper HIM before I go, I will,' said the

Dragon, and he leapt forward.

'R-U-U-U-N!' shouted Hiccup, but everybody was already running, as fast as they could.

In the distance, Hiccup could see four hundred warriors from the tribes of Hooligan and Meathead coming towards them from the Highest Point. They must have wondered at the boys' absence and come out to find them.

But they won't get here in time, thought Hiccup, *and even if they do, what can they do?*

Just then, the Dragon landed with a crash on the cliff top and suddenly the sun was blotted out.

Twenty boys ran towards the shelter of the ferns.

The Dragon picked up the nearest with one claw and turned him over.

It was Dogsbreath. By the time the Dragon had tossed him aside, muttering 'Not you', the other boys had disappeared into the bracken.

The Dragon was sick, but he laughed weakly. 'You're not safe there, oh no, for though I can't see you to kill you, I *can* use my... FIRE!'

The bracken caught fire with the Dragon's first breath and the boys ran out of it as fast as they could.

Hiccup stayed in a little longer because he knew

the Dragon was waiting for him.

Finally the heat became unbearable and he took a deep breath, closed his eyes and ran out into the open.

He had run hardly a hundred metres before two of the Dragon's talons closed around his middle and he was lifted up. Way, way up, so the other boys looked like little specks beneath him.

The Dragon held Hiccup up in front of him. 'We are BOTH Supper now, little Supper,' he said, and he tossed Hiccup high, high into the air.

As Hiccup somersaulted for the second time he thought to himself, *Now* THIS, *this really* IS *the worst moment of my life*.

Then he was falling.

He looked down. There was the Dragon's mouth, wide open like a great, black, cavernous tunnel.

He was going to fall into it.

17. IN THE MOUTH OF THE DRAGON

Hiccup fell into the Dragon's mouth and its teeth snapped shut behind him like prison doors.

He was falling through complete darkness, surrounded by a smell so awful it was suffocating.

He jerked to a sudden halt as the back of his shirt caught on something and held.

Hiccup hung there in the darkness, swaying gently. By a thousand to one chance his shirt had caught on a spear still stuck in the Dragon's throat since his Roman banquet. Hiccup's foot brushed against the wall of what he presumed was the Dragon's throat. The Dragon's digestive juices stung like acid, and he snatched his foot away.

Above him, Hiccup could hear the Dragon's great tongue sloshing and lunging about his mouth, trying to find Hiccup so he could crunch him to death... He hadn't intended to swallow him whole.

A disgusting river of green goo dripped down the puffy red insides of the Dragon's throat. Just across

Hiccup hanging next to the fire holes

from where Hiccup was hanging, green-yellow steam was puffing out of two small holes in the slimy wall. Every now and then a small explosion sent little flickers of flame shooting out of the holes.

How interesting, thought Hiccup, who was strangely calm, because he couldn't quite believe that this was really happening. *Those must be where the fire comes from.*

Viking biologists had wondered for years where the fire that dragons breathed came from. Some said the lungs, others the stomach. Hiccup was the first to discover the fire-holes, which are too small to see with the naked eye in a normal-sized dragon.

Way down below him, Hiccup could hear the distant rumbling of singing from the Dragon's previous meal. *A Seadragonus Giganticus obviously takes a long time to digest*, thought Hiccup.

It was indeed still going strong:

> *'Humans can be bland,*
> *but if you have some salt to hand,*
> *A little bit of brine,*
> *will make them taste div-I-I-I-ne...'*

The spear was gradually bending over with Hiccup's weight. It was only a matter of time before it broke and he fell to join the breezy optimist in the stomach below...

What was worse, the fumes and the heat and the smell were starting to confuse Hiccup so that he no longer really CARED. The terrible noise of the Dragon's heart beating had entered into Hiccup's chest and forced his own heart to follow the same rhythm.

A Dragon has to live, after all, he found himself thinking. And then he remembered the Dragon's words to him as he stood on the cliff top: 'You'll find that you come round to my point-of-view once you're inside me...'

Oh no! thought Hiccup. *The Dragon's digestion! It's already working!*

'I need to live, I need to live,' he repeated to himself, over and over again, trying desperately to block out the Dragon's thoughts.

There was a horrible creaking noise as the stout Roman spear began to split in two...

18. THE EXTRAORDINARY BRAVERY OF TOOTHLESS

And that would have been the end of Hiccup, if it had not been for the extraordinary bravery of a certain Toothless Daydream.

Toothless, if you remember, had refused to join in the battle at Death's Head Headland. He was intending to fly off somewhere down the coast a bit and lie low till all was safe again, but he stayed at the Highest Point for a while, terrorising birds and rabbits.

He must have been having a lovely time doing this, for he did not hear the approach of Stoick and the entire Tribes of Hooligan and Meathead until Stoick grabbed him around the neck.

'WHERE IS MY SON?' asked Stoick.

Toothless shrugged his shoulders rudely.

'WHERE IS MY SON???' bawled Stoick with an awe-inspiring yell so loud that Toothless's ears trembled.

Toothless pointed to Death's Head Headland.

'SHOW ME,' said Stoick grimly.

Under Stoick's fierce eye, Toothless reluctantly flapped off towards Death's Head Headland, followed by the two Tribes.

They arrived just in time to see the Terrible Monster throw Hiccup high in the air and catch him in his mouth like a whelk.

So much for the Fiendishly Clever Plan, thought Toothless.

He was about to use the opportunity of Stoick's obvious distraction to sneak off to a place of safety when something stopped him.

Nobody knows what that something was.

It was a moment which changed the whole worldview of the Hooligan Tribe. For centuries we had believed it was impossible for dragons to consider a selfless thought or a generous action. But what Toothless did next is impossible to explain as being in his own best interests at the time.

All his fellow domestic dragons were now flying somewhere over the Inner Ocean. As soon as they heard Fireworm's cry of 'Desert!', those who were hiding in caves or between crevices or crouched in the ferns rose up in a great swarm and abandoned their former Masters as fast as their wings could carry them.

The wild dragons from Wild Dragon Cliff had left hours before.

But something kept Toothless from flying after them – maybe it was Stoick's heartrendingly powerless cry of 'N-N-NOOOOO!!!' that caused him to pause. Or maybe somewhere in that self-centred green dragon heart of his, he really was fond of Hiccup and grateful for the hours that he had spent looking after him, not shouting at him, telling him jokes and giving him the biggest and juiciest lobsters.

'Dragons are S-S-SELFISH,' argued Toothless to himself. 'Dragons are heartless and have no m-m-mercy. That's what m-m-makes us s-s-survivors.'

Nonetheless SOMETHING made him turn right

around and SOMETHING made him fold his wings back and fly like a dragon blur to the Great Monster on the cliff tops. Which *really* was *not* in Toothless's best interests, as I said before.

Toothless flew right up the Monster's left nostril and started flying up and down the inside of his nose, tickling it with his wings.

The Sea Dragon lunged up and down, wrinkling his nose like crazy and bellowing.

'A-A-A-AAAAAAAH...'

The Creature stuck his great talon up his nose in a disgusting fashion and tried to winkle out the tickling flea that was irritating him.

Toothless didn't quite get out of the way of the talon in time and it scratched him on the chest. He hardly felt it though, he was so excited, and carried on tickling regardless, dodging the probing dragon claw.

'A-A-A-A-A-A-A-A-A-AAAAAAAAH...' bellowed the Sea Dragon.

Meanwhile Hiccup was being thrown this way and that inside the Dragon's throat as it shook its head from side to side. He was trying desperately to hang on to the spear which was in danger of becoming dislodged any second.

'... CHOOOOOOOOOOOO!'

The Dragon finally sneezed and Hiccup, the spear, Toothless, and a great deal of perfectly revolting Snot were scattered over the surrounding countryside.

Toothless remembered, as he was shooting through the air, that boys can't fly.

He folded his wings and dived after Hiccup, who was rapidly heading towards the ground.

Toothless grabbed hold of Hiccup by the arm and tried to take his weight. Dragons' talons are extraordinarily strong and he was able to break Hiccup's fall, not entirely, but enough so that when Hiccup crashed into the heather he was travelling reasonably slowly.

Stoick came plunging frantically through the grass.

He picked up his son and faced the Monster, holding his shield over Hiccup's unconscious body.

Toothless hid behind Stoick.

The Green Death had recovered from his sneezing fit. He shuffled forwards, bleeding horribly from fatal wounds to his chest and throat. He lowered his terrible head till it was on a level with the cliff top, and his evil, yellow eyes looked straight at Stoick.

'Time to die for *all* of us,' purred the Green Death. 'You can't save his life now, you know. You are quite, quite helpless. My FIRE will melt that shield like butter...'

The Green Death opened his mouth. He slowly sucked in a breath. Stoick tried to grab on to chunks of heather to hold them fast, but Stoick, Hiccup and Toothless were being dragged slowly but surely towards the gigantic black tunnel that was the Monster's open jaws.

The Green Death paused for a moment before he blew out again, enjoying their terror.

'This is what h-h-happens if you don't listen to the Dragon Law...' shrieked Toothless to himself in horror, as he peered round the side of Stoick's cloak.

The Monster puffed out his cheeks and Stoick and Toothless waited for flames to consume them.

But no fire came out.

The Green Death looked very surprised. He puffed out his cheeks and blew a little harder.

And again, no fire.

He tried once more, and now his head seemed to be turning a strange purplish colour with the effort of blowing, and it seemed to be swelling, bigger and bigger, as if he was being pumped up with air from the inside.

The Monster had no idea what was happening. He thrashed around wildly and his eyes bulged larger and larger until with a bang that could be heard for hundreds of miles in every direction...

... the Green Death blew up, right in front of their eyes.

This may seem like some sort of miracle, or an intervention on the part of the gods. But in fact there is a logical explanation. When Hiccup was hanging in the Sea Dragon's throat, desperately repeating 'I need to live, I need to live' to himself, he had taken off his helmet and had plugged the horns as hard as he could into the fireholes.

It was a perfect fit.

So, when the Dragon tried to use his fire, the blockage caused a build-up of pressure that eventually grew so great that the Green Death simply exploded.

Now there were pieces of Dragon flying in all directions. Stoick and Toothless were incredibly lucky not to get hit by anything, standing as close to the explosion as they were.

But a single, burning Dragon Tooth, eight foot long (one of the Monster's smaller ones), exploded straight towards Hiccup. The boy had been dragged out from under the shelter of Stoick's shield by the intake of the Monster's breath, and was now lying on the ground a couple of feet in front of Stoick and Toothless, completely exposed.

Stoick caught the movement of the Tooth out of the corner of his eye and flung himself and his shield forward. Only a Viking could have got there in time. Shooting woodcock with a bow and arrow develops very quick reflexes.

So Stoick's shield *did* save Hiccup's life after all. If it had not been there, the Tooth would have impaled Hiccup like a prawn on a stick. As it was, it buried itself deep, deep, deep into the bronze centre of the shield, and quivered there, blazing with green-edged Dragon flames.

Stoick lifted the shield, terrified that the Tooth might have pierced through to his son. But Hiccup was unharmed. His eyes were open and he was listening for something. He was listening for a strange sound that seemed to be coming from the flaming tooth itself. It was the sound of wheezy, echoing singing, like the wind blowing through coral caves, and it went something like this:

'I tell the mighty Big Blue Whale,
his life is over soon,
With one swish of this armoured tail
I put out the sun and moon...
The winds and gales are quivering,
when I begin to roar,
The waves themselves are shivering
and trembling back to shore...'

'Listen,' said Hiccup, happily, just before he passed out. 'The supper is singing.'

19, HICCUP THE USEFUL

The four hundred Vikings that were now gathered on the cliff tops broke into wild cheering for Hiccup and Toothless.

They were a strange, barbaric sight, all covered in disgusting green Dragon Snot and Slime, but beaming and shouting with the wild delight of those that have just been saved from Certain Death.

All around them, the terrible fight that had just taken place devastated the landscape. A choking green-grey smoke was hanging around making it difficult to see, but great chunks of Death's Head Headland appeared to have been torn out by the fight. Avalanches of rock were piled up on the beach. The terrible mountainous corpse of the Purple Death lay in the deeper water. Bits of the Green Death's insides and bones were scattered all over the place, while large sections of the heather and ferns were still in flames.

However, by some extraordinary miracle, nearly all the Vikings and their dragons had survived the dreadful battle.

I say 'nearly all' because, when Toothless crept

forward to lick the face of his Master with a flickering,
forked tongue, Stoick noticed a ghastly wound on the
little dragon's chest, which was pouring with bright
green blood. The talon of the Green Death had
pierced the very heart of the supposedly heartless little
dragon.

Toothless followed Stoick's gaze and looked
down for the first time. He let out a squeal of terror
and fainted dead away.

♥ ♥ ♥

Two days later, Hiccup woke up, aching all over, and very, very hungry. It was late at night. He was lying in Stoick's own great bed. The room seemed to be crowded with a great deal of people. Stoick was there, and Valhallarama, and Old Wrinkly, and Fishlegs and most of the Elders of the Tribe.

There were dragons there too: Newtsbreath and Hookfang snapping and biting around Stoick's legs, and Horrorcow perched on the end of Hiccup's bed. (The dragons had flown back as soon as they heard the explosion and realised the Masters of Berk were Masters once more. Being dragons, they had given no explanation for their disappearance, but they did have the grace to look a little sheepish.)

'He's alive!' shouted out Stoick in triumph, and everybody began to cheer. Valhallarama gave Hiccup a rousing punch on the shoulder, which is the Viking mother's equivalent of a really big hug.

'We're all here,' said Valhallarama, 'willing you to wake up.'

Hiccup sat straight up in bed, suddenly very awake indeed. 'But you're *not* all here,' he said. 'Where's Toothless?'

Everybody looked shifty, and nobody would look

at Hiccup. Stoick cleared his throat awkwardly.

'I'm sorry, son,' said Stoick. 'But he didn't make it. He died just a few hours ago. The rest of the Tribe are giving him a Hero's Funeral at this very moment. It's a great honour,' Stoick continued hurriedly. 'He'll be the first dragon ever to be given a proper Viking burial—'

'How did you know he was dead?' Hiccup demanded.

Stoick looked surprised. 'Well, you know, the usual: no pulse, no breath, stone cold to the touch. He was quite clearly dead, I'm afraid.'

'Oh, HONESTLY, Father,' said Hiccup, in a frenzy of exasperation, 'don't you know ANYTHING about dragons? That could have been a SLEEP COMA, it's a GOOD SIGN, probably means he's healing himself.'

'Oh, Thor's whiskers,' said Fishlegs. 'They started that funeral half an hour ago...'

'We've got to stop them!' yelled Hiccup. 'Dragons are only fairly fireproof. They'll burn him alive!'

Hiccup leapt out of bed with amazing energy, under the circumstances. He ran out of the room and

out of the house, followed closely by Fishlegs
and Horrorcow.

♦ ♦ ♦

Down at Hooligan Harbour, the awesome ceremony
of the Viking Military Funeral was nearly coming to an
end.

It was an incredible sight, if Hiccup had been in
the mood for it.

The sky was crammed with stars. The sea was
glass-flat. The entire tribes of Hooligan and Meathead
were gathered motionless on the rocks, and every
single person was carrying a lighted torch in one hand.

Even Snotlout was there, trying to look solemn,
with his helmet off his head out of respect, and his hair
neatly brushed.

'Good riddance to the newt with wings,' he was
whispering slyly to Dogsbreath the Duhbrain, and
Dogsbreath sniggered.

'Serve him right for breaking the Law,' sneered
Fireworm to Seaslug, who was picking his nose on
Dogsbreath's shoulder.

A replica of a Viking ship had been put out to
sea, and was drifting swiftly away from the island of
Berk along the path of the moon's reflection, past the

weird shapes of Stoick and Mogadon's burnt-out fleet.

Hiccup could just see the small body of Toothless laid out in the boat. Beside him lay Stoick's shield, the Dragon's Tooth still stuck in it like a gigantic alien sword.

Gobber the Belch sounded a mournful signal on his horn. He was now completely recovered after his unexpected flight.

'P-P-PARP‼!'

Twenty-six of Stoick's finest archers, standing to attention at the right of the Harbour, lifted their bows into the air. Every bow was loaded with an arrow in flame.

'N-N-NOOOO‼!' yelled Hiccup, with the best yell he had ever yelled.

But it was too late.

The flaming arrows soared gracefully through the air. They landed on the ship and set it alight.

Some of the crowd on the shore had turned to look upwards, wondering who dared to disturb this most solemn ritual.

'HICCUP!' shouted Thuggory the Meathead, joyfully recognising the figure on the horizon. There

was a murmur of wonder
from the crowd, as they whispered
'Hiccup?' to each other, then shouting and
cheering and calling out his name louder and louder.

Snotlout's jaw dropped open. He looked
thoroughly disappointed to see Hiccup very
much alive and well. Snotlout could just about
take Hiccup as a dead Hero, but a *living* Hiccup
the Hero was going to be very much in the way…

Hiccup was watching the burning ship, tears
pouring down his face.

The boat tipped and Stoick's shield and the Tooth
fell into the water. Just as the last piece of the boat was
about to slip beneath the waves, to be
consumed by fire and water, the flames reared up about
twenty foot into the sky. And, shooting out of those
flames, wings spread wide like a Phoenix,
trailing fire from his tail like a comet, came… Toothless.

He soared high, high, high into the stars, leaving
a path of flame as he flew. He dived down, down,
down towards the sea, and swooped up at the last
minute, to cries of wonder from the spectators. Hiccup
was anxious that he might be in pain, until Toothless
zoomed low enough over his head for Hiccup to hear

the little dragon's rooster cry of triumph.

Whatever Toothless's faults may have been, you have to admire his sense of occasion. Common or Garden dragons are not normally known for their spectacular flying skills, but even a Common or Garden dragon on fire is a spectacle in itself.

Toothless burned through the night sky like a live firework, performing screaming fiery somersaults, and flaming loop-the-loops. The crowd, who only a moment before were expecting to mourn the deaths of both Toothless and possibly Hiccup, were now beside themselves, hysterically cheering as Toothless showered them with sparks.

At last the fire got too hot for him and Toothless

plunged into the sea to extinguish himself, only to
burst out again and fly straight to Hiccup's shoulder.
There he acknowledged the wild applause with solemn
bows to right and left, slightly spoiling his dignity
with the odd 'Cock-a-doodle-doo!' of smug self-
congratulation.

Stoick signalled to the crowd for silence, but
only so he could boom out the following speech at
full blast:

'Hooligans and Meatheads! Terrors of the Seas,
Sons of Thor and most feared Masters of the Dragon!
I feel humbled to present you with the most recent
member of the Hooligan Tribe. I give you my son –
HICCUP THE USEFUL!'

And the words 'Hiccup the Useful' came
echoing down from the hills behind and were shouted
back again by the cheering crowd, and were picked up
and carried on the night breeze, until the whole world
seemed to be telling Hiccup that maybe he was going
to be Useful after all.

And that, my friends, *that*, is the Hard Way to
Become a Hero.

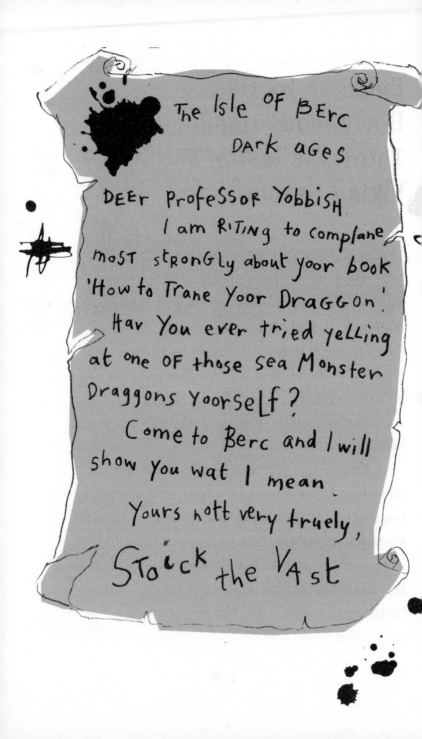

Epilogue by Hiccup Horrendous Haddock the Third, the last of the Great Viking Heroes

The story doesn't end there, of course.

The nineteen boys who entered Initiation with me those many years ago were all allowed into the Hooligan and Meathead Tribes as a result of their Heroic Actions in defeating two Seadragonus Giganticus Maximus in one day. The Battle at Death's Head Headland has passed into Viking legend and will be sung about by the bards while there are still bards to sing.

Of course, there are very few bards left nowadays. What is more, few have seen a Seadragonus Giganticus Maximus since, and people are already starting to disbelieve that such a creature could have lived. Learned articles have been written, suggesting that something that large simply could not have sustained its own weight. The dragons that would be my evidence have crawled back into the sea where men cannot follow and, what with Heroism being so unfashionable nowadays, nobody is going to believe the mere word of a Hero like myself.

But the thing about dragons – and I am a person who *knows* about dragons – is that it could very well be that they are merely *sleeping* down there in the black, black depths. There could be numberless numbers of them, all frozen in a Sleep Coma, with the unknowing fishes swimming in and out of their tentacles and hiding in their talons and laying eggs in their ears.

There may yet come a time when Heroes are needed once more.

There may yet come a time when the dragons will come back.

When that time comes, men will need to know something about how to train them and how to fight them, and I hope that this book will be more helpful to the Heroes of the Future than a certain book of the same name was to ME all those many years ago.

It is easy to forget that there were such things as these Monsters.

I forget myself sometimes, but then I look up, as I am looking up now, and I see in my mind's eye a shield, strangely changed by a rich encrusting of jewel-like barnacles and cold-water coral, with an eight-foot tooth sticking right out of the middle of it. I reach out and the edge of that tooth is still so bitingly sharp after all these years that just a gentle brush with the fingers might send a rain of blood down on these pages. And I bend my head, not too close, and I am sure I can just hear very, very faintly:

> 'Once I set the sea alight
> with a single fiery breath...
> Once I was so mighty that I thought
> my name was Death...
> Sing out loud until you're eaten,
> song of melancholy bliss,
> For the mighty and the middling
> all shall come to THIS...'

The Supper is still singing.

DRAGONS are ~~NEVER~~ Hardly ever grateful

"... which is Dragonese for...

THE END.

HOW TO TRAIN YOUR
DRAGON

How to Train Your Hogfly

written and illustrated by
CRESSIDA COWELL

~ CONTENTS ~

In the summer of 2002, a child digging on a beach discovered the How to Train Your Dragon papers: twelve books written by a Great Viking Hero known as Hiccup Horrendous Haddock the Third. But a recent astonishing discovery, deep in a cave in a small island off the west coast of Scotland, revealed many more 'lost' stories written by Hiccup, in both Old Norse and Dragonese.

And we can share the following short story for the very first time.

PROLOGUE BY HICCUP HORRENDOUS HADDOCK THE THIRD, THE LAST OF THE GREAT VIKING HEROES

Dragons should be as wild as the winds of the Archipelago.

But once, like my fellow Vikings, and before I knew any better, I trained dragons, rode them, fought beside them in battle. In fact, I had the reputation of being the finest dragon trainer and the most expert dragon whisperer that my Tribe had ever seen.

This is a story from a time in my life before the Great Dragon Rebellion, when the Wilderwest would be torn apart by a terrible fight between humans and dragons.

Life in the islands of the Barbaric Archipelago was nonetheless extraordinarily dangerous. In fact, it is a miracle that I ever made it into adulthood at all.

As you will see…

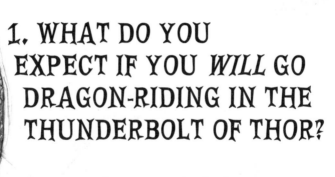

1. WHAT DO YOU EXPECT IF YOU *WILL* GO DRAGON-RIDING IN THE THUNDERBOLT OF THOR?

One misty afternoon in the Barbaric Archipelago, Hiccup Horrendous Haddock the Third was five thousand feet in the air, halfway along the Gorge of the Thunderbolt of Thor, flying on the back of his riding-dragon, the Windwalker.

This was not a good idea, and you shouldn't try it at home, for two excellent reasons.

Number One: I don't know if YOU have ever flown on the back of a dragon, but it isn't as easy as it looks. The wind gets in your eyes, and the higher you fly in the air, the harder it can be to hang on.

Number Two: flying a dragon is *particularly* dangerous if you are flying above the Gorge of the Thunderbolt of Thor, also known as the Slalom of Death. A windy, twisty slice of terror, cutting deep into the Mainland, this slalom needs a dragon-rider with razor-sharp reactions to avoid the pinnacles of rock that loom up unexpectedly through the mist.

Not to mention the Poison-darter arrows that shoot randomly from hidden holes, lower down in the cliffs.

And if you *do* happen to accidentally crash into one of those rock pinnacles and go spinning down, down, down, dizzily far into the bottom of the gorge; why, what will be waiting for you down there in the cold, grim, grey depths?

Throatgogglers, that's what. Throatgogglers have long necks that extend in and out of their bodies like adjustable telescopes, and they wrap these necks around their unfortunate victims and slowly squeeze the life out of them.

So they really are the sort of dragon that you should avoid at all costs.

Hiccup should have known better than to fly anywhere near the vicinity of a Throatgoggler, for

Hiccup was a clever little spidery twig of a boy, and a secret Dragonwatcher. Most Vikings considered intelligence to be a real downside in a properly barbaric Barbarian, but Hiccup was not like most Vikings.

Snuggled up in Hiccup's waistcoat, where it was nice and cosy, was Hiccup's hunting-dragon, Toothless. Toothless was a bright-green Common or Garden dragon, and one of the smallest hunting-dragons anybody has ever seen, before or since.

'Ooh, d-d-dear,' moaned Toothless, peering over the edge of the Windwalker's wing, down into the gorge below, where you could just about hear the greasy goggling gurgles of the Throatgogglers, a sound that chills the blood and makes every hair on your head stick up like the quills of a fretful porcupine.

'It looks ever-so s-s-scary down there. Why are we doing this again?'

Hiccup was the only Viking alive who could understand the language dragons speak to one another. So he replied to the little dragon in Dragonese, which

223

sounds most extraordinary when spoken by a human, because it is punctuated by odd popping and whooping noises for emphasis.

'It's a *race*, Toothless,' shouted Hiccup over the roaring of the wind, trying to sound as if he wasn't absolutely petrified, so as not to alarm the little dragon. 'We just have to fly down the gorge, touch the end and get back again. . .'

The race was called the Young-Warrior-in-Training -Dash-Down-the-Slalom-of-Death race, and was the last race in the Inter-Tribe Summer-tide Friendly BURY THE HATCHET Games. In the back of Hiccup's hood sat a lapdragon known as a Hogfly.

Hogflys are small, happy little dragons. This one looked like a round, very smiley miniature pig with long eyelashes.

Hogflys are incredibly optimistic and excitable, so this one wasn't frightened at all.

The Hogfly looked over the edge of Hiccup's hood at the wild, grim wilderness below and snuffled joyfully through its snouty nose.

'Oo!' huffed the happy Hogfly. 'Look at the pretty little doggies down there!'

Hogflys are small, HArpy little dragons.

224

'Those are not p-p-pretty little doggies,' said Toothless, coldly. 'They are Throatgogglers, and they kill on sight. Can't we get r-r-rid of this ridiculous Hogfly, Master? We could feed him to the Throatgogglers. . . ooo. . . *Let* Toothless! *P-p-please* let Toothless. . .'

Hiccup sighed.

Toothless had a bloodthirsty streak.

Look at the pretty little doggies down there!

'We're supposed to be LOOKING AFTER the Hogfly, Toothless. That isn't kind,' he replied. 'And as I said, we're not going to land down there, so it really doesn't matter. The most important thing is, we HAVE to win this race. . .'

Unfortunately, if you've ever read one of Hiccup's stories before, you will know that he spoke too soon.

Hiccup WAS going to land down there. He just didn't know it yet.

Hiccup's riding-dragon, the Windwalker, was an untidy, raggedy-looking beast, with a scared look in his eye. He hardly ever spoke, and when he did it was very softly and anxiously.

But despite looking like he'd been dragged through a hedge backwards, the Windwalker flew FAST. Steadily, quietly, he had stretched out his soft black wings, and he was catching up with the dragons ahead.

Hiccup's heart lifted with excitement as the Windwalker swooped faster and faster. Crouched down low, Hiccup almost felt he was a part of him as the Windwalker passed dragon after dragon.

'We're going to w-w-win! We're going to win!' Toothless was squealing.

In the lead, Hiccup could see Hullaballoo of the Danger-Brute Tribe, and Camicazi, heir to the Bog-Burglars, stretched out frontwards on her Rocket Ripper, slightly out of control but way ahead of the others.

'We *can* catch them, Windwalker. . .' Hiccup

whispered into his dragon's ear. 'You can do it. . . I *know* you can do it. . .'

Very soon, Hiccup and Windwalker had made so much progress that they had nearly caught up with a Devilish Dervish flying just in front of them. It was a great, muscly, shining creature, owned by Hiccup's cousin, Snotface Snotlout.

Snotlout was a massive, brutish bully of a boy with muscles bigger than pig's bladders and a mean look in his shifty eyes.

He was the son of Stoick the Vast's brother, Baggybum the Beerbelly, and he thought he would one day make a much better Chief of the Hooligan Tribe than Hiccup.

So he was always trying to get rid of Hiccup, for the good of the Tribe.

Snotlout was slightly held up by the fact that he was showing off, and riding his dragon standing up. This was very impressive, but it did mean he was travelling slower than he could have been.

The Windwalker got closer, closer. . .

. . . and the Devilish Dervish started to weave and turn, trying to prevent the Windwalker from overtaking them. Snotlout sat down, to gain more control over his dragon, urging the Dervish to go faster.

He looked over his shoulder, raging with temper to see Hiccup and Windwalker still there, however wildly he swerved. The Windwalker's scraggy wings were quivering at the edges, ready to make the move to get past him.

'Remember, Snotlout,' Hiccup shouted over to his

cousin. 'We're on the same side here! One of us *has* to beat the Danger-Brutes!' And then he whispered into the Windwalker's ear, 'Careful! Be ready to dodge in case he starts shooting at us.'

For when Snotlout was in a temper, he was perfectly capable of aiming a sneaky arrow or two at his cousin, particularly if he thought nobody might be watching.

But this time Snotlout had other plans.

'You may be OK at dragon-riding, Hiccup the Useless,' Snotlout shouted above the shrieking of the wind. 'But you'll NEVER have the Cold Heart of a Chief. . .'

Snotlout didn't reach for his bow and arrow.

Instead, he drew level with Hiccup.

Snotlout took something from his pocket.

It was an apple.

'Here, you silly Hogfly!' said Snotlout, smirking over his shoulder.

He waved the apple above his head to be sure the Hogfly saw it. 'Fetch!' he yelled.

And Snotlout threw the bright-green apple, down, down into the terrible greasy depths of the Gorge of the Thunderbolt of Thor.

Most dragons understand Norse, although they cannot speak it.

The Hogfly understood considerably less Norse than other dragons.

However, the Hogfly *did* know the word 'fetch'.

With a proud and joyful snort, it leapt out of Hiccup's hood. It barked once, twice, excitedly. . .

. . . and then it plunged down, down, down, into the gorge, speeding eagerly after the apple.

'Uh-oh,' said Hiccup, fighting to bring the Windwalker to a halt.

'A proper Viking leader would *leave him to die*,' snarled Snotlout, with narrowed eyes. 'But you're not a proper Viking leader, are you, Hiccup? Which is why *I* should be Chief one day, and not you!'

He watched as Hiccup fell behind, bringing the Windwalker to a rearing, mid-air halt.

And then Snotlout crouched down low over his Devilish Dervish, laughing, setting his sights on trying to catch up with Hullaballoo and Camicazi.

Leaving Hiccup dealing with a plunging, hysterical, halting Windwalker.

How do I get myself in situations like this one? thought Hiccup to himself, staring down over the Windwalker's bucking shoulder at the disappearing pink bottom of the Hogfly, its tail wagging like a jolly little flying bulldog, who was miraculously *not* being hit by Poison-darter arrows.

Zing! Zing! Zing! sang the nasty hiss of the arrows as they shot out from

every opening in the gorge walls while the terrible sound of the Throatgogglers' Death Gurgle drifted upwards:
Reeeooorgghhghhhgglegurglgowarghh uggle uggle URGH...

Viking after Viking passed Hiccup as he tried to steady Windwalker... There went Thuggory the Meathead, followed by Speedifist, and then Tuffnut Jr and Dogsbreath zoomed past. Until Hiccup's best friend, Fishlegs, an untidy daddy-long-legs of a boy, trying to stay on the back of an irascible little Chickenpoxer, and currently coming last in the Race, drew up alongside him just as he finally got Windwalker under control.

'What are you doing? Why have you stopped?' puffed Fishlegs. 'This is not the time to start admiring the view, Hiccup! You **HAVE** to win this race!'

'The Hogfly,' panted Hiccup. 'It's down in the gorge...'

Fishlegs halted the Chickenpoxer and stared down into the gorge, eyes bulging with absolute horror. 'H-hiccup...' he stammered. 'You're not going after it, are you? You have to leave it. It'll probably be fine!'

Hiccup's heart beat quick with terror, and his stomach sank lower than his furry boots. He was never going to have the Cold Heart of a Chief.

He couldn't leave the poor, silly little Hogfly to die a horrible death all on his own.

'I'm sorry, Fishlegs,' said Hiccup, sadly. 'I have to do this. . .' And then he gently nudged the Windwalker with his knees, pointing him down into the gorge.

2. THE UNTRAINABLE DRAGON

How *did* Hiccup get himself in a situation like this one?

Well, for once, it wasn't really Hiccup's fault.

It had all begun when Hiccup's father Stoick the Vast, the Chief of the Hooligan Tribe, O Hear His Name and Tremble, Ugh, Ugh, DIDN'T invite his cousins Very-Vicious the Visithug or Dastardly Dangerus, Chief of the Danger-Brutes, to the Inter-Tribe Summer-tide Friendly BURY THE HATCHET Games.

Stoick the Vast was excellent at growing a beard like a blown-up gorse bush. He was magnificent at charging at the enemy while roaring like a bull with bellyache. But he was not the Brightest Barbarian in the Business.

'They'll NEVER find out,' he said to himself.

Hiccup, Stoick's son, was a small, ordinary-looking boy with arms like two pieces of spaghetti and a worried expression.

'If Very-Vicious the Visithug and Dastardly Dangerus find out we're having a Games and we haven't invited *them,* they'll declare a Blood Feud on us,' Hiccup had said, when he found out that Stoick hadn't included

235

these terrible chieftains in his invitation.

'Hiccup.' Stoick the Vast had held up a solemn hand. '*I* am the Chief, so *I* make the decisions around here. Luckily, I am a bit of a genius in the politics department. Tact and foresight, Hiccup, being a Chief is all about tact and foresight. The Visithugs and the Danger-Brutes are completely out of control, and they're always spoiling things. Look at what happened a couple of years ago when they burnt down the Grims' Great Hall for a joke! And I haven't invited EVERYONE,

I am the Chief, and...
Luckily, I am a
bit of a genius
in the politics
department.

have I? I *had* to invite the horrible Uglithugs because we're doing one of the races in their territory, and they have those notices up saying: "Trespassers Will be Killed Horribly But Mercifully Quickly if They Are Lucky." And I didn't invite the Murderous Tribe, either. . . or the Lava-Louts. . . or the Hysterics. . .'

'Yes, but, Father. . . the Danger-Brutes and the Visithugs are FAMILY, so they'll expect an invitation,' Hiccup pointed out. 'They'll be terribly offended if they get left out. And isn't there something in the Barbaric Code about how you have to invite family to a Games?'

'Hiccup.' Stoick had leant forward and patted his son on the shoulder importantly. 'Take it from your father. They're very *distant* family: we're barely related at all! And they will NEVER find out. I told everyone to keep their invitations strictly underneath their helmets. And the Danger-Brutes and the Visithug Tribes tend to go hunting in the summertime.'

'Yes, but, Father. . .'

'Not another word,' said Stoick the Vast.

So that was how Chief Stoick the Vast woke up on the morning of the Games to find his bedroom full of Visithug warriors, and Very-Vicious the Visithug's axe held lovingly to his throat.

Stoick kept his eyes closed in the pathetic hope that if *he* couldn't see THEM, *they* couldn't see HIM. '*Uh-oh. . .*' he gulped to himself. '*They found out. . .*'

Now, the thing about the Tribes of the Archipelago was that some Tribes were scarier than others. The Peaceables, for instance, weren't scary at all, poor things; and nor were the Quiet-Lifes or the Silents. The Hooligans, the Meatheads, the Bog-Burglars and the Bashem-Oiks were all your average Vikings, burglars and pirates of course, and always bashing each other up and stealing each other's deer, but basically fairly good-natured in a hopeless sort of way.

UH-OH...

But Tribes like the Uglithugs, the Murderous, the Hysterics, the Berserkers, the Outcasts, the Danger-Brutes and the Lava-Louts – ah, these Tribes were a different matter indeed.

They were all pretty majorly terrifying.

And one of the most terrifying Tribes of all was the Visithugs. They had an unpleasant habit of drinking out of their enemies' skulls after sacrificing them to the Sky Dragons on the pointiest peak of Mount

Thuggery, and this made them difficult to like.

Very-Vicious the Visithug was six feet tall with a beard so out of control that it looked like his chin was being attacked by a runaway bison.

He had so many notches on his sword to mark the Vikings he had killed that he had to get his mother, Brenda the Barbarian Blacksmith, to make him a new and bigger sword.

'Hello, there, Stoick the Small,' smiled Very-Vicious, with satisfaction. 'I've heard that you've invited all of the Tribes of the Archipelago to an Inter-Tribal Games, and you haven't invited ME. It's a little rude of you, I must say, particularly as my uncle twice removed on my father's side married your grandfather's sister, Honking Henrietta. . . I considered us practically brothers!'

'Of COURSE I invited you!' spluttered Stoick, feeling the cold blade on his neck. 'You were the first on my list. . . my favourite relation! The invitation must have been lost in the post. . . the Dragon Mail has been terrible lately!'

'Us Visithugs are very keen on manners,' hissed Very-Vicious. 'We always apologise before we hang a victim over a cliff by his fingertips. . . We are careful to

raise a toast respectfully to the spirit of our enemy when
we are drinking out of his skull. . . We never forget to
wipe our feet before we burn a house down. That's what
makes us so lovable.'

Hmmmm. . . gulped Stoick, thoughtfully.

'And what you have done here, Stoick, is. . . well,
you have hurt my feelings. . .' said Very-Vicious, and
he smiled an unpleasant smile with a lot of black and
broken teeth in it.

'I'm so sorry, Very-Vicious,' said Stoick the Vast. 'I
didn't know you HAD any feelings.'

Oh, dear.

Only one thing could happen when Very-
Vicious's feelings were hurt.

'BLOOD FEUD!'
yelled the Visithug hordes,
waving their axes around
happily.

'Now, I am tempted to
kill you right here, and that
would teach you not to hurt
my feelings ever again,' said
Very-Vicious. Stoick gulped
again.

241

'However,' said Very-Vicious, removing his axe from Stoick's neck for a moment, and picking his teeth with it thoughtfully, 'as I am very soft-hearted I will overlook your rudeness if you do me a tiny favour.'

'What would that be?' asked Stoick, holding his neck and heaving a sigh of relief.

'You have a revolting little son called Hiccup, do you not?' said Very-Vicious.

'Now, this is all MY fault! Let's leave my son out of it, shall we?' said Stoick, uneasily.

'HICCUP, YOU REVOLTING LITTLE WORM!' shouted Very-Vicious. 'GET IN HERE, YOU HORRIBLE LITTLE HOOLIGAN HEADACHE!'

Hiccup wandered in, half asleep.

He blinked at the bedroom full of Visithugs, and his heart sank slightly lower than his sandals. But he managed to say politely, 'Why,

Hiccup wandered in, half asleep.

Very-Vicious the Visithug. . . Assorted muscly and violent Visithug warriors. . . What a lovely and unexpected surprise! Have you come for breakfast?'

'We have not come for breakfast.' Very-Vicious smiled. 'We have come to kill your father.'

'Ah,' said Hiccup, looking carefully around the room.

Twenty-six Visithugs, all armed to the teeth with swords, axes, daggers and knuckle-dusters, versus his father: unarmed and only in his hairy underpants, and Hiccup himself, also unarmed, and a little undersized for a Viking as it was.

This was going to be tricky.

Not IMPOSSIBLE, perhaps, but tricky.

'However, I have decided to give your father a chance to keep his life. *We* are going on a little hunting expedition over in the Peaceable country. . .'

'Deer?' asked Stoick, his eyes brightening, for he did love a deer hunt.

'Peaceables,' said Very-Vicious evilly. 'They look so funny when they run.'

'Oh. . .' faltered Stoick. 'That's not very nice. . .'

'No,' admitted Very-Vicious. 'It isn't.' He paused, before continuing: 'I have heard that your son Hiccup here is something of an expert dragon trainer,' said Very-Vicious. 'And *I* have this amazing untrainable dragon. So, while we are gone, I will leave my untrainable hunting dragon here on Berk, and when we come back from this Peaceable hunt, I will expect *your son* to have trained it for me.'

'Or else?' asked Hiccup, a cold, unpleasant sensation making his stomach churn.

'Or *else*,' smirked Very-Vicious, 'I will a) declare a Blood Feud on account of my cousinly feelings being

hurt and b) remove your father's Hooligan head from his Hooligan shoulders because, as you know, according to the Barbaric Code, if a cousin fails to invite another cousin to a Games like this one, said cousin can remove the other cousin's head from his shoulders and display it on the wall of his Chiefly Hut.'

Hiccup swallowed hard.

Uh oh, uh oh, uh oh.

That Barbaric Code really was, well, a little. . . *barbaric*.

And if a terrifyingly tough Chieftain like Very-Vicious couldn't train this dragon, it must be something really quite out of the ordinary.

'But *if* you train my dragon, and make him as obedient as my other hunting-dragons here,' Very-Vicious said with a grin, waving at a couple of dragons larger than panthers standing to military attention on either side of him, 'I give the Word of a Chief, your father will live.'

'In which case,' said Hiccup, thoughtfully, 'I accept the challenge.'

'Bravo!' mocked Very-Vicious. 'A wise choice. He's a very bright lad, your son. Excellent!'

Very-Vicious clapped his great paws together. 'This

is a Win-Win situation for me. I either have your ugly great mug on my wall, Stoick, or I have a lovely obedient hunting-dragon. . .'

It sounded like a Lose-Lose situation as far as Stoick was concerned.

Very-Vicious whistled between his front teeth, and yelled, 'COME OUT, Hellsbells!'

UH OH, UH OH, UH OH, thought Hiccup, as he waited anxiously for this Untrainable Hunting-Dragon to walk through the door. In his head he ran through all the ghastly possibilities. . .

A Rottviper? A Rawripper? One of those new types of Gory-Gummed Gronckles?

'I SAID, COME OUT, HELLSBELLS!' shouted Very-Vicious, and then threw back his head and gave such a truly scary, inhuman roar that, frankly, most dragons would have obeyed, and terrified the horns off Hiccup.

Hiccup and Stoick exchanged horrified glances.
WHAT COULD THIS DRAGON BE?

Oh, my goodness, with a name like Hellsbells, it couldn't be a Hellsteether, could it?

After an extremely tense couple of moments of nothing happening, Very-Vicious gave a sigh of exasperation, and opened the flap covering the bag hanging around his waist and. . .

. . . a very tiny dragon *indeed* poked its nose out of Very-Vicious's bag, snuffled a few times, and then buzzed up and into the air.

It looked like a happy little pig.

It was a Hogfly.

Stoick and Hiccup blinked at the Hogfly in astonishment.

It was small.

It was pink.

It had very long eyelashes and tiny talons and teeth.

Somehow it didn't seem like the kind of dragon a truly scary Chieftain like Very-Vicious the Visithug ought to have.

But Very-Vicious was so very, very scary, Hiccup and Stoick didn't dare laugh.

Very-Vicious stroked the Hogfly under its chin, making grunting, cooing noises. 'There you are, my little diddums. . . who's Daddy's little darling, then?'

The Hogfly batted its eyelids and gave a small snuffly woof.

'Right,' said Very-Vicious briskly. 'If anything

happens to this dear little dragon, I will personally kill not just Stoick but the whole of the Hooligan Tribe, with my bare hands. We'll be back in a couple of days or so and we'll expect it to be perfectly trained. Otherwise it'll be BLOOD FEUDS and heads off all round. . .'

'BLOOD FEUD!' yelled the Visithugs, waving their axes around and launching themselves forward excitedly.

'Not now, guys,' explained Very-Vicious. 'Only when they fail the task.'

'No problem!' beamed Stoick the Vast. He suddenly felt a whole lot better, and in fact was nearly BURSTING with the effort not to laugh. 'Hiccup will train this. . . er. . . *terrifying beast*. . . in no time! Can I give you and your warriors breakfast before you go off on your travels?'

Very-Vicious made a face. 'No, us Visithugs can't eat your revolting porridge. We've got loads of pigs-brains-mixed-with-mouldy-haddock as a delicious packed snack.'

And the Visithugs trooped out of the door, leaving a whole load of bloody footprints on the floor and a most unpleasant smell that lingered for a good couple of days afterwards.

They had barely left when Stoick the Vast exploded

with great booming laughter.

'HA HA HA HA HA HA HA!'

He clapped Hiccup on his back.

'Shhh father, they might hear you. . .'

Stoick calmed down, and rubbed his hands
together.

'Phew,' boomed Stoick the Vast. 'I was really
worried there for a moment. I thought it would be one
of those new Gory-Gummed Gronckles. You'll have that
silly little animal trained in no time. Who'd have thought
Very-Vicious would have a beast like that one?'

Stoick gave a chuckle, and
stomped out.

'Oh dear,' said Hiccup,
looking at the Hogfly. 'Oh
dear, oh dear, oh dear, oh dear.'

oh
dear,

3. TRAINING THE HOGFLY

One hour later, and Hiccup had explained his problem to his best friend, Fishlegs. 'Well, *I* don't see the problem,' said Fishlegs.

They were both looking at the Hogfly.

'It doesn't look very vicious, does it?' he continued. 'Your father's probably right: you'll train it in no time. Look how you trained Toothless!'

'I wouldn't say that Toothless was PERFECTLY trained,' said Hiccup. (Toothless was, at that very moment, in the corner eating one of Hiccup's Aunt Gladioli's hats.) 'But that's not the difficulty. . .'

Hiccup lowered his voice, in case he hurt the Hogfly's feelings. 'The issue is,' he whispered, 'that Hogflys get the wrong end of the stick about *everything*, and this makes them virtually untrainable.'

The Hogfly looked up at Hiccup with big, soppy eyes.

'Woof!' The Hogfly beamed. 'Woof!'

'You see?' whispered Hiccup. 'It thinks it's a dog.'

Hiccup turned to the Hogfly.

'Hello, Hogfly,' he said.

'Hello, Grandma!' barked the happy little Hogfly. It licked Hiccup's hand.

'I am not your grandma,' corrected Hiccup, gently. 'But I am a friend. A good friend. Do you want to play a game?'

The Hogfly was so over-excited it zigzagged in tiny, snuffling, zooming circles in the air, tripped over its own tail and fell in the fire. (Luckily, Hogflys are fireproof, so it didn't hurt itself.)

'Happy birthday!' chirruped the Hogfly, eyes beaming with good-natured cheer as Hiccup rescued him from the fire.

'Oh dear,' sighed Hiccup. 'Do you know what this is, Hogfly?' He picked up an apple from the table and showed it to the Hogfly. The Hogfly flapped over to it, and sniffed it all over. 'Ooo yes, yes, yes, yes, yes, yes!' huffled the Hogfly, excitedly. 'It's a snail! It's a chair! It's a doormat! It's a rabbit!'

'It's an apple,' said Hiccup. 'Normally you would eat it.'

'I'll eat it!' squealed the Hogfly, pink in the face with excitement, wings blurring madly like an overgrown hummingbird. 'I'll *eat* it!'

It tried to *sit* on the apple in the air.

'OK. . .' muttered Fishlegs. 'I'm beginning to see your problem. . .'

It tried
to SIT on the apple. . .

'I'll eat it!' squeaked the Hogfly joyously again, patting at the apple with its wings, turning upside down and doing a headstand on top of it.

'You don't *need* to eat it. . .' said Hiccup, patiently. 'I'm just going to pretend this apple is a ball. . . Look! And I'm going to throw it in the corner. . . and *you're* going to fetch it. . .'

'Hooray!' screamed the Hogfly. 'See you soon! It's bath time! Hello, Mother!'

Hiccup threw the apple into a corner of the room.

The Hogfly was so excited it forgot to breathe, and turned purple in the face, its bottom wiggling madly. Green smoke came drifting out of its ears, there was a loud explosion, and the Hogfly shot three feet backwards, before diving into a nearby cauldron that was full of deer stew and rescuing a parsnip. It then zoomed upwards, the parsnip trailing from its mouth and, for no obvious reason, ran across the ceiling upside down. It landed in front of Hiccup and Fishlegs, dropping the soggy, collapsing parsnip at Hiccup's feet, before turning over in the air and presenting its tummy to be tickled.

Toothless had stopped eating Aunt Gladioli's hat in order to watch this performance.

'W-w-what,' asked Toothless disapprovingly, 'is *that?*'

Hiccup sighed.

He tickled the Hogfly's tummy, and the Hogfly squirmed and giggled with delight, before leaping up and licking Hiccup's face all over with its large slobbery tongue.

'It's a Hogfly,' explained Hiccup, in between licks.

'Well, t-t-tell it to go away!' howled Toothless, grabbing the Hogfly by the tail, and trying to stop it licking Hiccup. 'This is Toothless's house, and we don't need another d-d-dragon!'

'*That* is the most untrainable dragon I have ever seen in my entire life,' said Fishlegs. 'You have a MAJOR problem.'

'I know,' said Hiccup, despondently.

4. THE INTER-TRIBE SUMMER-TIDE FRIENDLY BURY THE HATCHET GAMES

The Inter-Tribe Summer-tide Friendly BURY THE HATCHET Games began about lunchtime that day, with all the Tribes gathering in Hooligan village for a large banquet. Camicazi, a Bog-Burglar, with hair so wildly tangled it looked like a couple of porcupines having a fist-fight, was a good friend of Hiccup and Fishlegs. She ran across the bracken, greeting them both with a joyful shove as they hadn't seen each other in a while.

'This will mark a NEW ERA in the life of the Archipelago!' cried Stoick the Vast to the assembled crowds as he gave a welcoming speech. 'The end to

Blood Feuds between us all. . . And to symbolise the friendship between our peoples I would like to invite you all to. . .

'BURY YOUR HATCHETS IN THE HEATHER!'

With joyful snorts and bellows, the Hooligans and the Bog-Burglars and the Meatheads and the Bashem-Oiks and all of the other supposedly friendly Tribes took to burying their weapons. (Being Vikings, they couldn't resist turning it into a competition as to Who Could Bury Their Hatchet the Deepest, of course. . . but nonetheless, it was a step forward, on their part.)

'Excellent, excellent!' Stoick the Vast beamed, rubbing his hands and striding over to Hiccup and Fishlegs and Camicazi, as all around the Vikings bustled about, unloading barrels and setting up tents and cooking equipment. 'What an excellent idea of mine this little competition is,' he said. 'At this rate Blood Feuds will be a thing of the past! And in the meantime, I was quite right all along about *not* inviting the Visithugs and the Danger-Brutes. They really do spoil everything. . .'

'But we haven't heard from the Danger-Brutes yet, and I'm making absolutely no progress in training Very-Vicious's dragon, Father!' Hiccup pointed out, anxiously.

GORY-GUMMED GRONCKLES

~ STATISTICS ~

COLOURS: Brown and lime or yellow-green
ARMED WITH: Sticky, slippery drool
FEAR FACTOR: 6
ATTACK: 6
SPEED: 4
SIZE: 6
DISOBEDIENCE:................8

Baby Gronckle napping inside shell

'If I don't train him in *the next few days*, Very-Vicious is going to claim your head!'

Hiccup was trying to teach the Hogfly to 'sit', but, to Camicazi's amusement, the Hogfly thought this meant digging a large hole in the ground.

But Stoick wouldn't listen to Hiccup.

'Pooh!' he said, waving an airy hand. 'I've never heard such nonsense! You really do worry too much, Hiccup. One large YELL and you'll have that silly little Hogfly in order. And we haven't heard from the Danger-Brutes yet because they haven't found out we're having the Games in the first place. As I always say, you have to leave the politics to me, as I have so much experience, and—'

'Hang on a second. . .' Hiccup interrupted him, staring up at the sky. 'What's that?'

'By the Whiskers of Woden!' said Stoick, in a gobsmacked sort of way. 'It's the *Danger-Brutes*! They must have found out! And they're heading straight for the house! *Stop!* Dastardly Dangerus! *Stop!* You're going to crash into the—'

Too late.

BOOM!

The most enormous Rhinoback dragon crash-landed *bam splat* in the middle of Stoick's Chiefly Hut-on-Stilts, taking out the entire left side, including Stoick's handsome new bed. The Rhinoback carried on downward, landing on its feet in the bog below, completely unharmed, before folding its wings delicately and trotting forward, stopping in front of Stoick, who was watching, frozen with horror.

'My HOUSE!' boggled Stoick the Vast, mouth opening and shutting like a bamboozled haddock. 'My beautiful new HOUSE!'

A man the size of a brick wall with a cunning expression and a considerable number of swords climbed off the back of the Rhinoback.

Dastardly Dangerus the Tenth, Chief of the Danger-Brutes, was less scary than Very-Vicious the Visithug – MOST people were less scary than Very-Vicious the Visithug – but he was still big and horribly muscly and he was *crafty* and very annoying.

'Whoops.' Dastardly smiled, looking over his shoulder and surveying the destruction with satisfaction.

My HOUSE!' boggled Stoick the Vast

Chief Dastardly
Dangerus the Tenth

'Shame. That was a nice Chiefly Hut. But some people might say that this serves you right, Stoick, YOU OLD *VILLAIN!*' he snarled suddenly, holding the pointy bit of one of his swords in Stoick's direction. 'Why was *I* not invited to these so-called Inter-Tribe Summer-tide Friendly BURY THE HATCHET Games? *AM I NOT YOUR FRIEND?*'

Hiccup tugged desperately at his father's waistcoat, whispering urgently, 'Father! Remember! Don't forget, you're trying to bury the hatchet here! *Stay calm!*'

For Stoick had swelled up like a large, infuriated, six-foot-bullfrog-that's-about-to-burst.

With a magnificent effort, Stoick dragged his eyes from the ruined remains of his Chiefly Hut and resisted the urge to bonk Dastardly on the nose.

That really wouldn't have been friendly. And it

would have started exactly the sort of fist fight that the Inter-Tribe Summer-tide Friendly BURY THE HATCHET Games had been designed to prevent.

'Well, we couldn't invite *everyone*, Dastardly,' said Stoick, from between gritted teeth. 'There wouldn't be room on the island! The Outcasts aren't here. . . or the Murderous. . .'

'The Uglithugs are here and everyone hates *them*!' objected Dastardly Dangerus.

The Uglithugs gave grunts of outrage.

'And my second cousin twice removed on my father's mother's side married your grandmother, Buffintruda the Beautiful, the one who was known as the Flower of Bashem!' snapped Dastardly. '*Some people might say that this is no way to treat* FAMILY!' he spat, eyes narrowed. '*Some people might say that you were deliberately insulting our cousinship! Some people might say that such an insult is a perfectly good reason to start another. . .* BLOOD FEUD!'

BLOOD FEUD!!

'BLOOD FEUD!' joyfully roared the rest of the Danger-Brute Tribe, landing their own Rhinobacks all over the village, making a terrible mess of the heather.

Shouting 'BLOOD FEUD!' in the middle of a gathering of the Tribes of the Archipelago is a bit like shouting 'CHICKENS!' in the middle of a hungry gathering of foxes.

A restless murmur of discontent went around the once joyful village.

'Blood feud!' whispered a rogue Bog-Burglar. A Bashem-Oik lobbed his oyster sandwich at a Meathead's ear.

People started surreptitiously dropping to their knees and scrabbling at the heather to *un*bury their axes.

The whole situation looked like it could get rapidly out of hand.

'Yes, I know, I know, Dangerus,' said Stoick, wearily. 'In order to avoid the Blood Feud, according to the Barbaric Code, you want me to offer you my Hooligan Head instead. . .'

'Excellent. . .' drawled UG the Uglithug, cruel eyes lighting up as he caressed his sword. 'A little blood-letting might get these Games off to a good start. . . How *kind* of you to offer, Stoick. . .'

264

Hiccup stepped forward and held up a hand.

'Can we just talk about this *peacefully*?' he said, soothingly. 'Chief Dastardly Dangerus the Tenth is a much more sophisticated, cunning and inspired villain than Chief Very-Vicious. I'm sure he won't insist on doing something as obvious as removing your head, Father, if you let him join the Games?'

'Won't he?' said Stoick, dubiously.

Dastardly Dangerus paused a moment, stroking his beard.

Hmmm. Cunning! Sophisticated! The shrimpy little Hooligan boy did have a point. Dastardly prided himself on his villainy, of course he did, but he felt he was a far more original and devious scoundrel than that old-fashioned Very-Vicious.

And, as Hiccup suspected, Dastardly was secretly dying to join in the Games, so that he could show off.

Dastardly Dangerus smiled a smile as tricksy as a boatload of weasels. 'You probably didn't invite us in the first place, Stoick, because you were AFRAID we'd beat you into the middle of next week, and so we shall!' he sneered.

'Afraid?' yelled Stoick, outraged. '*AFRAID?* OF COURSE I WASN'T *AFRAID!*'

'In which case,' smiled Dastardly, putting his sword away, and looking very crafty, 'maybe there's a way we can avoid any bloodshed. Your son is right. Perhaps I'll overlook the insult, if I join in the Games and we make a little bet?'

'ANY BET YOU LIKE!' yelled Stoick.

'If we Danger-Brutes join in these Games of yours and we BEAT you,' said Dastardly cunningly, 'I get to choose any dragon of yours to keep. . . and vice versa, in the unlikely event that we lose.'

'I ACCEPT YOUR CHALLENGE!' cried Stoick the Vast, and the two chieftains bumped bellies on the bet.

'Oh, Father. . .' sighed Hiccup, his heart sinking. Because the truth was, the Danger-Brutes were frighteningly fit, and really quite good at Burglary, the Dragon Sprint, Tossing-the-Grandmother, Lying, Spitting and pretty much all of the Barbarian blood sports.

Plus they cheated.

'Name the dragon you will choose in the EXTRAORDINARILY slim chance that you win.' Dastardly smiled again.

'Your Rhinoback!' cried Stoick the Vast, terribly

pleased with himself. It was almost worth having to build his Chiefly Hut again to get his hands on Dastardly's Rhinoback, a fine fighting animal.

'Very good,' purred Dastardly Dangerus. 'And I choose. . .'

His voice lowered in greedy glee. 'The Silver Phantom.'

Stoick the Vast's great belly slipped down like a collapsing balloon.

Tricked! He had been tricked.

'But the Silver Phantom belongs to my wife, Valhallarama!' he protested.

Tricked!
He had
been tricked.

'But the Silver
phantom belongs
to my wife
Valhallarama!'

The Silver Phantom was Valhallarama's pride and joy, an extraordinarily rare species that was the shining jewel of the dragon world. 'I'm not sure Valhallarama would hand over the Silver Phantom to anybody. . . she's away Questing. . .'

Nor was Stoick as sure as he would like that if it was a choice between him and the Silver Phantom, which one Valhallarama would choose.

'Of course she would choose *you*, Father,' said Hiccup, reading his mind and patting his hand sympathetically.

But at that moment. . .

'Daddy!' cried a small, sleepy voice from the top of Dastardly Dangerus's Rhinoback.

Dastardly Dangerus gave a start, put a large finger to his lips and whispered furiously to Stoick, 'Shhhhh! You've woken up the precious. . .'

The precious?

Dastardly Dangerus lifted down a small girl with red hair who had been sitting behind him on the Rhinoback.

The little girl pointed at Stoick. 'Who ith that hairy man, Daddy?' she asked.

'That's Stoick the Vast, precious,' cooed Dastardly,

soothingly. 'He's a very rude cousin of mine and we're going to beat him and his Tribe in these Games and then I get to choose whichever dragon of his I want. . .'

The little girl considered this.

'I want *that* one,' she said, pointing at Toothless.

'Which one do you mean, Nettle, my love? *This* one?' roared Dastardly Dangerus, picking Toothless up from Hiccup's helmet, where he was perching and looking down disapprovingly at the Hogfly, still digging his hole.

'Are you sure?' he said, in disappointment. 'Not the Silver Phantom?'

'Yeth!' exclaimed the little girl, delightedly holding out her hands. 'He'th tho thweet!'

'Toothless is not sweet!' howled Toothless furiously, as Dastardly's fingers handed him, struggling wildly, to the little girl. 'Toothless is F-F-FEROCIOUS!' He began struggling in Nettle's arms like a conger eel caught in a lobster pot. 'No hugging!' he cried as the little girl cuddled him so tightly he nearly choked. 'No kissing!' he yelled, and when she ignored him, bit her on the finger.

269

No hugging!
No kissing!

But Nettle seemed delighted.

'Look! He'th kithing me back!' squealed the little girl happily.

'That wasn't a KISS, you horrible human!' yelled Toothless. 'That was a BITE! Let me go!'

'You shouldn't be treating this dragon like it is some kind of pet, Nettle,' said Camicazi disapprovingly. 'Look at Stormfly here. She's a wild animal, she just hangs out with me because she chooses to.'

The little mood-dragon turned a bright golden yellow in approval, and tossed her head. 'I wouldn't stay if I didn't want to,' she agreed, eyes gleaming.

But Nettle wasn't listening to Camicazi. She gripped on to Toothless even tighter.

Toothless finally wriggled his way out of the little girl's embrace, and flapped out of reach, screaming down insults at her in Dragonese, while she looked up at him adoringly.

A stern light came into the little girl's eyes.

'That'th the dragon I want, Daddy. Heeth tho cute. I thall call him Thweetie.'

'Sweetie?' hissed Toothless, in fury. 'Sweetie? Someone t-t-tell the horrible little girl I am a T-t-toothless Daydream, not a Sweetie!'

'No problem, precious,' sighed Dastardly, twirling his axe. 'If that's the one that you want, that is the one you shall have. Watch out, Stoick. . . We Danger-Brutes are going to beat you at EVERYTHING. . .'

'Phew,' said Stoick the Vast, as Dastardly Dangerus stomped off. 'That was a close one! For a nasty moment I thought we were in trouble. . .'

Toothless and Hiccup glared up at Stoick reproachfully.

'Yes, I know, I'm sorry about *Clueless,* Hiccup. . .' Stoick coughed. 'But you have to admit, he wouldn't be much of a loss to the Tribe, not like the Silver Phantom.'

'He'd be a loss to *me*,' said Hiccup, sadly.

'And, anyway, we're going to beat those Danger-Brutes in the Games, NO PROBLEM!' Stoick shouted over his shoulder as he hurried after Dastardly.

'Of course you will!' said Camicazi. 'You're way better than those walruses!'

'The Danger-Brutes *cheat*, though,' said Fishlegs, gloomily. 'It's hard to beat

The Danger-Brutes
CHEAT, though

cheaters. And I'm still worrying about what's going to happen when Very-Vicious comes back and finds out you *haven't* trained the Hogfly.'

This was turning into a very bad week.

Stoick could still lose his head, and Hiccup could lose Toothless.

Oh dear.

Camicazi

and her hunting dragon, Stormf

5. THE YOUNG-WARRIOR-IN-TRAINING-DASH-DOWN-THE-SLALOM-OF-DEATH

The week didn't really improve much.

Hiccup, Fishlegs and Camicazi made absolutely no progress in training the Hogfly. Hiccup tried to warn Stoick of this, but Stoick was so busy trying to prevent Blood Feuds from breaking out between the Tribes that he wasn't really listening.

The Bog-Burglars beat everyone at Burglary, Tossing-the-Grandmother and Lying, which made the Bashem-Oiks so cross that they remembered their Blood Feud with the Bog-Burglars over a spilled pint, and Stoick had to let them win at the Spitting contest in order to stop war breaking out. Mogadon the Meathead accused the Danger-Brutes of cheating in the Arm-wrestling and one of the Bashem-Oiks was in a huff because his grandmother was twice the size of everyone else's, which made Tossing-the-Grandmother an unfair contest.

All in all, Stoick was absolutely exhausted with playing the peacemaker, and thoroughly regretting he had ever had the clever idea of holding the Games in the first place.

Worse still, by the end of the week, the Uglithugs were in first place, followed by the Bog-Burglars, but because of the Danger-Brutes' cheating the Hooligans and the Danger-Brutes were *tied*.

The fate of Toothless was going to come down to whether a Danger-Brute or a Hooligan finished fastest in the last race, which was the Young-Warrior-in-Training-Dash-Down-the-Slalom-of-Death.

So, on the last day of the Games, Toothless was panicking.

'Don't let me go to the h-h-horrible little girl. . .' poor Toothless wept, flinging his arms around Hiccup's neck and refusing to let go. Hiccup patted him consolingly, but the truth was, he was pretty anxious himself. He couldn't imagine a life without Toothless, maddening though the little dragon could be sometimes.

'Don't worry, Toothless,' said Hiccup, in a determined way. 'We will win this race.'

'You won't beat ME.' Camicazi grinned.

Hiccup looked around. Camicazi was the finest dragon rider in the Archipelago.

'Maybe not,' admitted Hiccup. 'But I can beat the Danger-Brutes.'

'Don't get me wrong, Hiccup, I admire your optimism,' said Fishlegs. 'It's just that everybody else will have Rocket Rippers. Windwalker is a lovely dragon and everything, but he only has three working legs and he's a bit. . . well. . . *clumsy.*'

It was true: the Windwalker's limbs had grown so much recently, he almost seemed to have lost touch with them, like a colt learning to walk, and one of them was bundled up with bandages. And the starting horn tended to make him launch himself thirty feet backwards in fright.

'Windwalker is still a young dragon,' Hiccup said, buoyantly, 'but he's getting older and stronger and quicker. And I've got a secret ingredient to make his shaggy skin a bit more aerodynamic.'

♦ ♦ ♦

Two hours later, roaring and bellowing with excitement, the Tribes of the Archipelago gathered on Long Beach for the final event of the Inter-Tribe Summer-tide Friendly BURY THE HATCHET Games.

'YOUNG WARRIORS! GATHER ROUND WHILE I EXPLAIN THE RULES!' bellowed Gobber the Belch, head of the Pirate Training Programme on Berk.

The young Meatheads, Hooligans, Danger-Brutes, Bog-Burglars and warriors from other Tribes gathered around Gobber, their riding-dragons whirling and nipping above and around them, with the adults watching and cheering from the edge of the beach.

'The last event in these Games is a fun little Dragon Sprint called the Young-Warrior-in-Training-Dash-Down-the-Slalom-of-Death!' roared Gobber the Belch. 'Only Warriors-in-Training can compete in this one. The race begins at the Long Beach, heading east to the Uglithug territories, down the Gorge of the Thunderbolt of Thor, and back again. The race will start when I blow my horn!'

He jauntily waved a long silver horn over his head. 'REMEMBER!' he bellowed in a jolly fashion. 'Anyone who flies too low runs the risk of *Certain Death*, because

276

in the cliffs of the gorge are the Poison-darter arrows. Anyone who flies to the left or to the right of the gorge will face *Certain Death*, for those are the Uglithug territories. And anyone who is foolish enough to fall off or enter the depths of the gorge will face—'

'—Certain Death?' asked Fishlegs, politely.

'That's right, Fishlegs!' said Gobber with merry enthusiasm. '*Certain Death*. For down in the gorge lurk the THROATGOGGLERS, some of the nastiest species of dragon in the Archipelago!'

'Of course they are!' muttered Fishlegs. 'Which is why, entirely for FUN, us Vikings are flying right above their territory instead of staying at home composing a little poetry in the bath. . .'

'No pulling, no shooting, no shoving, no cheating, no spitting and the first Young Warrior-in-Training back wins!' cried Gobber.

Dastardly Dangerus's fifteen-year-old daughter Hullaballoo, Nettle's elder sister, was six feet tall and built like a barn door, while all of the other Young Warrior-in-Training Danger-Brutes were similarly tough.

Every single one of them had either a Rocket Ripper, a Rageblast, a Tornado or a Devilish Dervish dragon.

'The Hooligans haven't a chance!' roared
Hullaballoo, pointing at Hiccup and Fishlegs. 'Look at
those funny little warriors at the end!'

'That toothless hunting-dragon is YOURS,
Nettle!' guffawed Dastardly Dangerus, laughing so hard
his helmet fell off.

HA HA HA HA HA HA HA HA HA HA HA!

The merry laughter of the Young Warriors-in-
Training from all the Tribes rang out across the beach as
everyone turned to look at Hiccup and Fishlegs.

They were, it had to be admitted, a slightly ridiculous sight.

Fishlegs had outgrown his Chickenpoxer to such an extent that his feet actually touched the ground when he sat on her. And Hiccup's secret ingredient to make the Windwalker more aerodynamic had been to slick the Windwalker down with Goredragon Goo. Which unfortunately also made him look like a bedraggled, sopping-wet cat that had been out in some slightly sticky rain.

Maybe this wasn't such a good idea, thought Hiccup, sliding about on the Windwalker's back. It felt as if he was trying to sit on a bar of soap.

Toothless, the smallest hunting-dragon anyone had ever seen, and the little pink Hogfly didn't add much 'cool' factor, either.

'Ooh, they're cheering!' exclaimed the Hogfly in delight. 'Hooray!' it said, clapping its little paws together.

'They're not cheering, you f-f-foolish dragon,' hissed Toothless. 'They're *laughing* at us. . .'

'Hiccup, what have you done to your dragon?' said Stoick, stepping forward and muttering into Hiccup's ear. 'You realise, son, the importance of us winning the race, don't you? Not only might you lose *Shoeless*, here, but more importantly, the honour of the Horrendous Haddocks is at stake. We can't have the other Tribes laughing at us.'

'Yes, Father,' said Hiccup, who had been slowly sliding to a forty-five degree angle while Stoick made this speech. 'But Windwalker is faster than he looks.' Hiccup shook his fist, and looked determined, slightly undermined by the fact he was nearly horizontal to the ground.

'IT'S ALL DOWN TO THIS RACE, AND PREPARE TO *LOSE*, STOICK!' yelled Dastardly Dangerus.

'MY SON SAYS HIS DRAGON IS FASTER THAN IT LOOKS!' roared Stoick, loyally.

Hiccup's thighs couldn't hang on any longer, and he slowly slipped around the Windwalker's body so that he was hanging upside down from the dragon's tummy.

'Great stance, Hiccup!' sneered Snotlout, pleased that Hiccup was making a fool of himself. 'Look, guys, he's so good he's going to beat those Danger-Brutes upside down!'

HA HA HA HA HA HA HA!

Fishlegs helped Hiccup up just in time for the starting horn.

PARRPPPPP!

Windwalker shot thirty feet backwards in alarm, while everyone else launched into the air; even Fishlegs, although he had to run along the ground a bit first, before the Chickenpoxer could take off. . .

The race had begun.

6. THE GORGE OF THE THUNDERBOLT OF THOR

We are nearly back where we started, at the beginning of Chapter One.

The Young Warriors-in-Training set off, swooping low over the ocean towards the east. Hiccup started last, because Windwalker had been so alarmed by the starting horn, but by the time they got to the edge of the gorge, Hiccup had already overtaken Fishlegs, and many of the other Young Warriors-in-Training, one by one.

You know the next bit.

Hiccup caught up with Snotlout, and Snotlout threw the apple down, down, down into the gorge.

And Hiccup halted the Windwalker, letting all of the other Young Warriors overtake him, until finally, a horrified Fishlegs, who had been all the way in the rear, caught up.

'L-l-leave it!' shrieked Toothless, plastering himself over Hiccup's face and looking deep into his eyes. 'It'll be fine! We got to win the r-r-race! Throatgogglers is k-k-killers! Toothless don't want to d-d-die!'

'We can't leave it!' yelled Hiccup, hauling on

the reins to put Windwalker into a dive. 'You know perfectly well it won't be fine! You said it yourself, Throatgogglers are killers. . .'

'But we don't c-c-care about the Hogfly!' screamed Toothless. 'We only care about TOOTHLESS!'

'Well, *I* care about the Hogfly!' shouted Hiccup, as he finally got the reins correctly positioned in his hands.

Poor, terrified Windwalker dithered for a moment. Every fibre of his being was shouting, 'DON'T GO INTO THE GORGE OF THE THUNDERBOLT OF THOR!'

But the Windwalker, for all his nerves and anxiety, was a brave and noble creature at heart. Despite his terror, he folded back his shaking wings and went into a dive, following after the tiny pink blob that was the Hogfly, who was shooting into the nightmare of the gorge with happy woofs.

Into the danger of the canyon the busy little Hogfly buzzed, barking happily to itself: 'FETCH! Hogfly FETCH! Ooh. . . hello, doggies. . .'

The depths of the Thunderbolt of Thor were a glorious but rather unnerving sight, all drifting mist and oozing grey-green sludge at the edge of a rushing river.

The Throatgogglers were in a listless mood, recovering from a long hunting expedition. It was their hatching time, so the females were sitting on their eggs, in large nests balanced precariously on pinnacles of rock jutting out of the torrent of the river. The nests were made out of tangled, burnt branches from trees, and thatch stolen from nearby Quiet-Life fishing villages. The males wallowed sleepily in the boggy boundary of the river, cooling their furnace-like bodies, submerged up to their crocodile eyelids, every now and then yawning, showing off terrifying lines of jagged, razor-sharp teeth. A sickly yellowy-green mist curled off the heat of their scales as they lolled in the cold of the mud.

At first, the Hogfly had the advantage of surprise.

The Throatgogglers weren't used to entertaining visitors, down there in the splendid privacy of their own special crevasse.

And you can't really blame the Throatgogglers for being carnivores, it was just in their nature, but if any dragon as small and round and delicious as this one were to pay them a call, they had usually been dragged there in a state of complete terror and hopeless panic.

They certainly weren't buzzing around joyfully, making happy, snuggly snuffles like the unsuspecting Hogfly.

'Woof woof woof!' squeaked the Hogfly. 'Quack! MIAOW! Hello, mud! Hello, grass! Hello, ugly great doggies with huge pointy teeth!'

The Throatgogglers followed his bumblebee path with their astonished yellow eyes.

'We're playing a game!' chirruped the Hogfly, zipping madly through the bulrushes. It landed on a Throatgoggler's head, licked its amazed face all over and buzzed off again before the Throatgoggler had got over the shock of it.

'Last one there's a peanut! I'll chop you into smithereens, you cowardly sons of jellyfish!' (This was

clearly a phrase learnt from Very-Vicious himself.)

'It's bedtime! Hello, Mother! Where's the biscuit?' By this time the Hogfly had thoroughly confused itself and so it did a couple of enthusiastic somersaults in the air, chasing its own tail, dived into the bog and charged out again shrieking, 'WOAH, THAT TICKLES!'

As the Hogfly hovered in the air, looking around itself, bright-eyed, the Throatgogglers were beginning to wake up to what was happening, and extend their long necks out of their bodies.

One huge panther-like creature, shaking the mud off its wings and sharpening its claws, moved smoothly through

the mud towards the Hogfly, drawling in an evilly sinister hiss, '*What game did you say you were playing, brother?*'

'Oh. . .' said the Hogfly, stopping uncertainly for a moment. '**I can't remember!**'

At this perilous moment, there was a shout from behind the Hogfly.

It was Hiccup, on the back of the Windwalker, desperately trying to warn the little lapdragon.

'**DON'T STOP! HOGFLY, WATCH OUT BEHIND YOU!**' Hiccup howled, as the Windwalker swerved this way, that way, dodging the alligator jaws of the Throatgogglers launching themselves out of the mud at them as they flew.

But Hiccup was too late.

The Throatgoggler had caught the little dragon by the wings.

'**Let ME guess the game! Let ME guess!**' the Hogfly mused, putting an affectionate paw on the hungry creature's lower jaw, still under the unfortunate impression that the Throatgoggler wanted to play. '**I Spy?**' said the Hogfly. '**Trick or Treat?**'

'**Treat, I think.**' The Throatgoggler smiled as it uncurled its neck even further, ready to wrap that neck round the Hogfly and squeeze all the breath out of it, like a gigantic boa constrictor.

'And I love you too,' whispered the Hogfly, kissing the Throatgoggler on the nose.

At that very same moment, one of Hiccup's arrows caught the Throatgoggler in the back of the neck.

It didn't make much more of an impression than an ant bite on the creature's tough hide but the mixture of this scratch and the surprise of the kiss was enough to make it drop the Hogfly with a yelp.

The Hogfly zoomed out of reach, shrieking, 'I know the game! I know the game! The game is . . .

. . . FETCH!'

The little dragon turned a full somersault in the air in its delight in having remembered.

'AND THERE THE APPLE IS!'

The Hogfly had caught sight of something round and green lying under the tail of a nearby snoozing female Throatgoggler. It zoomed over, buzzing busily, his tail wriggling like that of a merry little piglet, and started burrowing under the Throatgoggler's sleeping bottom, trying to 'fetch' the green thing.

'ŊOOOOOOOOOOOOOOOO!' yelled Hiccup, zigzagging through snapping Throatgoggler mouths. (Luckily the Goredragon Goo came in useful here, for one Throatgoggler got hold of Windwalker's leg but it slipped out of the Throatgoggler's grasp like butter.)

'That's not an *apple*, Hogfly,' shouted Hiccup. 'That's an *EGG*!'

Hiccup pulled the Windwalker to a tight, wing-flapping halt, made a desperate grab to snatch the Hogfly away. . .

. . . but he was too late.

The Hogfly had yanked the egg out from under the mother Throatgoggler's bottom with such force that it woke her up. She launched herself in outrage at the Hogfly, but by some miracle the Hogfly skipped out of reach, squeaking joyfully to itself in triumph and pride.

'Hogf'y, *fetch!* Hogf'y. . . *fetch!*' (Although with its mouth full of egg it sounded more like, 'HourfEEE! HoerfeEEEK!')

Bellowing like an infuriated bull, the mother Throatgoggler charged after the Hogfly. The Hogfly dodged out of the way, squealing delightedly, like it was playing a game of 'Tag'.

'DROP THE EGG!' howled Hiccup. 'The mother Throatgoggler is after her EGG! DROP IT and she'll stop chasing you!'

But although Hiccup HAD managed successfully to get the Hogfly to 'fetch', he had never been able to get it to 'drop'.

'DROP! DROP! DROP!' Hiccup shrieked as he flew after the Hogfly, twisting the Windwalker this way and that in a slalom through the gorge, pursued by the howling mother Throatgoggler.

The Hogfly merely clamped its mouth tighter and tighter around the egg, squeaking with pleasure, and miraculously avoiding the Throatgoggler jaws and the Poison-darter arrows, until one snapping bite of the mother Throatgoggler was so close that it nipped one of his titchy wings.

The tip snapped off, not enough to stop the Hogfly

flying, but enough for it to really *hurt*.

'Oo!' shrieked the Hogfly. 'Ow!'

. . . and then something seemed to click in its chirpy brain.

'Oh. . .' breathed the Hogfly. Its curly tail drooped and it flew on as fast as it could, looking back at the scary, scary gorge and the terrifying panther-like mother dragon pursuing it, her eyes gleaming.

Finally realising the trouble it was in, the little Hogfly faltered a smidgen, slowing in its fear.

OH... breathed
the HoGFly.

The mother Throatgoggler's eyes lit up. This was more like it. . . This was how victims normally reacted when caught in their territory. . . It was only a question of one quick snap of the jaws. . .

The poor Hogfly was mesmerised by fear, looking over its shoulder, shaking so hard it was flying slower and slower. . .

'FLY, HOGFLY, FLY!' screamed Hiccup, who had

finally caught up with the little dragon.
'IT'S A GAME, AND THEY CAN'T
CATCH YOU!'

'Oh, it IS a game!' said the Hogfly in relief. 'I
KNEW it!' And just as the mother Throatgoggler was
about to get it in a crunching lunge, Hogfly dashed off
singing, 'Can't catch me-e-e-e-e. . .' (Which sounded
like, 'EEEE ee eeeee. . .')

'Can't catch yo-o-ouuuuuu. . .' Hiccup sang back,
in encouragement, as the Windwalker and the little
buzzing Hogfly flew alongside each other.

It was a desperate flight all right, and only the
Hogfly's belief that it was all a jolly game was saving
their lives.

Hiccup finally caught the giggling, rolling Hogfly,
grabbing and putting it firmly under one arm as he tried
to remove the Throatgoggler egg from its jaws, but the
little Hogfly. . .

. . . would . . . not. . . let. . . go.

'K-k-kill him!' begged Toothless. 'Can we kill
him?'

Eaarrrawwwwww!

They had reached the top of the gorge now, and
they shot up, out of the chasm, with the terrible cliffs on

either side, and into the clear blue sky above. But the mother Throatgoggler meant business, and was flying straight up towards them, out of the gorge too.

In her desperation to catch up with her egg, she was finally gaining on them, even with Windwalker at 'Blur Speed'.

Hiccup had a brainwave.

Around his waist there was a small bag, full of the apples that he had been using to try and train the Hogfly over the course of the week.

The Hogfly was still tucked under his arm, but he had given up trying to break the Hogfly's stubborn grip on the Throatgoggler egg.

Instead, Hiccup reached into his bag and took out one of the training apples.

'Here!' he called over his shoulder to the mother Throatgoggler. 'Have your egg back!'

And then he threw the apple down, down into the gorge. Now, the mother Throatgoggler would normally not have been fooled by such a trick, even though the Throatgoggler egg does look remarkably like a big green apple.

However, in a state of motherly concern for what

she assumed was her egg, now dropping down at great speed towards the bottom of the gorge, she gave a shriek of alarm, folded back her wings, and dived down after it.

'Let's get out of here!' yelled Hiccup, and pointed the Windwalker towards home. 'Eventually, she's going to realise we've still got her egg. . . Hogfly, WILL YOU LET GO OF IT, or those Throatgogglers will follow after us if we don't give it back to them!'

But the Hogfly would not drop the Throatgoggler egg, however much Hiccup begged.

Now that they were out of the nightmare of the gorge, Hiccup could see the little flying specks of the other Young Warriors, in the distance, way beyond the Island of the Quiet Life, halfway back to Berk already.

They were too far in front for Hiccup to catch up now.

But Fishlegs, on his Chickenpoxer, was flying in the other direction, back towards Hiccup.

Fishlegs had had the most horrible half-hour. The Chickenpoxer had refused to descend into the gorge after Hiccup, and so poor Fishlegs had spent the time flying back and forth just above where Hiccup and the Hogfly had disappeared, trying to spot what had happened to them, not sure what to do.

'Oh, thank Thor! You're ALIVE!' Fishlegs grinned in total and absolute joyful relief when he got level to Hiccup, turning around to fly back beside him. 'I thought you were dead for sure that time. . . How did you get out of THAT one?'

'I'm not quite sure we're out of it yet. . .' panted Hiccup, looking over his shoulder once more as they raced towards the distant outline of the island of Berk, on the horizon.

For although he was desperately relieved that he and Toothless and the Hogfly and the Windwalker had emerged from the gorge in one piece, Hiccup was dreadfully shaken, and he was certain that the danger was not over.

However, the Hogfly was delighted with itself.

'Peep yeek work! Peep yeek work!' sang the Hogfly, its mouth still full of Throatgoggler egg. (Which meant, 'I won the game! I won the game!')

'But we've lost the race,' groaned Hiccup. 'Hullaballoo of the Danger-Brutes is going to finish ahead of us.'

From the depths of Hiccup's backpack came a sad voice. 'Toothless is D-D-DOOMED. . .' said Toothless, from the bottom of the backpack. 'Toothless will never see the M-m-master ever again. Toothless will have the little girl who calls him SWEETIE for a Master. . . Is the end of the WORLD. . .'

Well, it wasn't quite the end of the WORLD, but the idea of losing Toothless made Hiccup feel very sad and bleak indeed. What would he do without that naughty, warm little dragon, sleeping on his feet every night like a small, flammable water bottle? How had he ever lived without Toothless in his life?

When they finally flew into the skies above Berk, Hiccup still couldn't see any dragons launching out of the Gorge of the Thunderbolt of Thor. Maybe the mother Throatgoggler was still searching for her egg down there? Maybe she hadn't worked out that Hiccup had tricked her, so the Throatgogglers wouldn't pursue them?

But Throatgogglers were renowned for being exceptionally protective of their eggs, and Hiccup had a horrible feeling he hadn't seen the last of them.

THROATGOGGLERS

~ STATISTICS ~

COLOURS: Vivid colours but can dim them when attacking

ARMED WITH: Long extendable necks

FEAR FACTOR: 8

ATTACK: 8

SPEED: 7

SIZE: 8

DISOBEDIENCE: 9

7. HOW TO KEEP YOUR HEAD

By the time Hiccup finally landed back on the Long Beach on Berk, he was in a bedraggled, woeful state, covered in slimy gorge water, clothes torn by dragon arrows.

'And, last of all. . .' cried Gobber the Belch, 'comes Fishlegs No-Name on his dragon, Chickenpoxer, and Hiccup Horrendous Haddock the Third, on his dragon Windwalker!'

'Bad luck, loser-boy,' drawled Snotface Snotlout.

Stoick the Vast's great belly had dropped in a crestfallen way. Nobly, he tried to conceal his disappointment at Hiccup's failure. 'Never mind, son,' he said. 'Winning isn't everything. . . That little Bog-Burglar Camicazi won the race – and she is,' admitted Stoick grudgingly, 'the finest bareback dragon rider I have EVER seen, apart from your mother Valhallarama, of course – but Hullaballoo of the Danger-Brutes came second, and that does unfortunately mean that the Danger-Brutes have beaten us...'

'Yes, Father,' said Hiccup, sadly. 'But we may have another, even worse problem. . . I had a small confrontation with some Throatgogglers in the Gorge of the Thunderbolt of Thor, and. . .'

But before Hiccup could explain that there was
a possibility that thousands of Throatgogglers could be
about to invade Berk. . .

. . . there was a great roaring cry from above.

'HELLSBELLS! LITTLE DIDDUMS!' shouted
Very-Vicious, as the Visithug Tribe descended on their
great Rhinobacks and Razorwings. 'COME TO DADDY,
MY LITTLE PINK BABYKINS!'

With a squeal of delight at seeing Very-Vicious, the
Hogfly wriggled in Hiccup's arms with such energy that
Hiccup let go. The lapdragon zoomed up to greet his
hairy, sweaty, terrifying Master with every appearance of
delight.

And, some twenty feet up in the air, the Hogfly
finally dropped the Throatgoggler egg.

Before he could even think, Hiccup was running
forwards, his hands out, ready to catch the egg, as it
plunged down towards a rather rocky bit of the beach
below – where if it landed it might break, for Hiccup
didn't know how fragile Throatgoggler eggs were. . .

Hiccup wasn't very good at Bashyball, but he
launched himself forward and made a very impressive
attempt at a catch. . .

. . . missing the egg, which landed on the rocks.

To Hiccup's relief, the egg bounced straight off them, one, two, three times, and came to a sludgy halt in the sand.

Trembling, covered head to foot in sand because he had landed rather heavily on his tummy, Hiccup got to his feet and checked the egg for cracks. It was fine, thank Thor, with not even a hairline fracture on its gorgeously shiny bright-green surface.

There was something sticking to it, though, some sort of oddly shaped stone, but it came away when Hiccup brushed it off, so it must have just been the Hogfly's saliva that had stuck it to the egg.

It seemed Throatgoggler eggs were pretty robust after all. *I must remember to put that in my* Guide to Dragons and Their Eggs, Hiccup thought.

He carefully put the egg and the oddly-shaped stone in the bag at his waist, along with the apples that the egg so closely resembled. *Maybe I could go back and return the egg to the Throatgogglers?*

He felt terrible about accidentally stealing their egg from them, even though technically that was the Hogfly's fault, not his.

Meanwhile, up in the air. . .

302

Who's Daddy's little darling?

'Welcome back, my liddle sweetie-pie!' cooed Very-Vicious, cuddling up to the Hogfly as he steered his Razorwing down to land on Long Beach.

'Oh, for Thor's sake,' moaned Stoick, 'I'd forgotten about the Visithugs. . . Very-Vicious! My dear cousin. . . I hope you are well?'

Very-Vicious vaulted off the back of his dragon, and his mood changed bewilderingly quickly from cooing adoration at the Hogfly to dangerous fury at Stoick.

'I am not very well at all, Stoick, you treacherous burglar!' fumed Very-Vicious, shaking his axe. 'I strongly suspect you Hooligans told the Peaceables we were coming! You have completely ruined my week. . .'

'N-nooooo. . .' stammered Stoick.

But, in fact, Very-Vicious was correct in his suspicion. Hiccup had sent a Dragon Mail message to the Peaceables warning them that the Visithugs were going to make a surprise attack, and so the Peaceables had jumped in their ships to make for their summertime territories.

The Visithugs had had a very boring time stalking SHEEP, which is not half as fun to a Visithug as chasing Peaceables.

'I am going to be very disappointed if this delightful but untrainable little Hogfly of mine is not properly trained!' shouted Very-Vicious. 'I gave the Word of a Chief that I would take off your head if he isn't, and I am in just the mood for taking off heads!'

'Of course it's trained, isn't it, Hiccup?' said Stoick in a harassed sort of way, looking at the Hogfly wriggling excitedly in Very-Vicious's arms.

'Woof, woof!' barked the Hogfly. 'Run for your lives! Call the cavalry! Last one there's a peanut!'

'GATHER ROUND!' yelled Very-Vicious, placing the Hogfly gently down on the sand. 'LET US SEE WHETHER THE WEIRD LITTLE HEIR TO THE HOOLIGAN TRIBE REALLY HAS TRAINED

MY CHARMINGLY CUTE BUT UNTRAINABLE
DRAGON!'

A gigantic crowd, chattering and laughing, gathered
round in a huge circle, with Hiccup and the Hogfly in
the middle of it.

'Oh, this is going to be good,' sneered Snotlout,
his eyes alight with malice. 'Now they will see how
they should have asked ME to train the Hogfly, not the
Useless. . . And *I* would have used a WHIP. . .'

'I haven't had very long to do this, remember,' said
Hiccup, nervously.

'SILENCE!' roared Very-Vicious, waving his axe
around. 'Show me my dragon is trained or I remove your
father's head RIGHT NOW!'

'Come on, Hiccup, my boy,' said Stoick, eyeing
that axe. 'I think Chief Very-Vicious means what he
says, and I'd like to keep my head. . . I'm really rather
fond of it.'

What could Hiccup do to make Very-Vicious
and the Visithugs think he HAD actually trained the
untrainable little Hogfly?

Hiccup thought about the Throatgoggler egg and
the training apples in his bag. A Throatgoggler egg really
did look remarkably like an apple. If he could fool a

mother Throatgoggler, perhaps he could trick a whole load of muscly but credulous Vikings. . .

A Ridiculous but Cunning Plan came to him. One that might just work.

'Hogfly,' said Hiccup. 'Hogfly!'

'Hello?' replied the Hogfly, politely. 'Is someone at the door?'

Hiccup reached into his left pocket. He drew out an apple and showed it to the crowd, so that they could all see it.

He then threw it about three feet in front of him, and called, 'Fetch, Hogfly, fetch!'

The Hogfly's eyes lit up with triumph.

It knew what *this* meant!

The Hogfly barked three times: 'Woof! Woof! Woof!' and fetched the apple, its little curly tail waggling like billy-o with pride.

There was a silence of gobsmacked astonishment.

And then. . .

HA! HA! HA! HA! HA! HA! HA! HA!

laughed the Tribes of the Archipelago.

WOOF! WOOF!

'They're cheering! They're cheering!' whooped the Hogfly, bowing in the air, turning almost red with pride.

'They're *laughing*, you f-f-foolish reptile,' sighed Toothless, poking his nose out from Hiccup's waistcoat.

Very-Vicious the Visithug's eyebrows descended in fury.

'I am assuming,' he said, silkily, 'that you are not making fun of the Visithug Tribe? This is not evidence of a properly trained hunting-dragon. This is the kind of trick that you could train a DOG to do. . .'

'Chief Very-Vicious the Visithug,' said Hiccup, stuttering a little. 'You wanted this dragon trained as well as your other hunting-dragons. That is the task you set me to perform.' He cleared his throat, nervously. 'Well, then, let us see whether THEY can do this trick. If they can, why, then I have failed in the task. . .'

Very-Vicious's eyes gleamed with pleasure. 'Prepare for your father's Hooligan head to be removed from his Hooligan shoulders!' he cried.

Stoick gave a great gulp, and rubbed his neck thoughtfully.

Silence on the beach.

'What are you doing, Hiccup?' whispered

Camicazi. '*Any* dragon can fetch. . . it's the first trick we teach them.'

Very-Vicious snapped his fingers. His hunting-dragon, Jagtooth, swooped down in a blur of military precision and snapped to attention.

But this time, Hiccup did not throw an apple for Jagtooth to fetch.

He reached into his bag and drew out the Throatgoggler egg instead.

Hiccup threw the Throatgoggler egg about three feet in front of him.

'Fetch!' said Hiccup, calmly.

HA HA HA HA HA HA! roared the crowd, for this really was a laughably easy task for any normal hunting-dragon.

Very-Vicious leant forward eagerly.

Jagtooth looked at the Throatgoggler egg. . .

. . . and his great, shining, obedient body began to shake.

'Fetch!' yelled Very-Vicious, in a frenzy of fury. 'Fetch! Fetch, fetch, fetch, *fetch*, FETCH!'

The crowd was silent again, this time in amazement.

Jagtooth just stood there, shaking, until finally the

great military weapon gave a small miaow, like a baffled kitten, spread his great wings, and flew off.

'Fetch,' said Hiccup to the Hogfly, who was talking to its own reflection in a puddle, under the impression that it was another Hogfly.

'Fetch!'

Only a Hogfly would be silly enough to fetch a Throatgoggler egg.

The Hogfly gave two happy, eager barks, and fetched the egg, dropping it at Hiccup's feet.

NOW the crowd erupted in genuine applause, as the Hogfly bowed in every direction.

'RIGORMORTIS!' bellowed Very-Vicious to another of his terrifying hunting-dragons. 'FEEEEETCHHHHH, OR I'LL TURN YOU INTO A HANDBAG!'

But Rigormortis would not fetch. With an apologetic wave of his wings, he too, flew away to hide.

One after another, all of Very-Vicious's hunting-dragons refused the simple task, while the Hogfly obligingly did it again and again and again, to the massive cheering of the appreciative crowd, delighted to see the Visithug Tribe making fools of themselves.

'I don't believe it. . .' hissed Snotlout. 'I DO NOT

believe it. The Useless is getting away with it again. . .
It's a trick. . . It's a trick. . . It MUST be a trick. . .'

Well, well, well.

'You see, Chief Very-Vicious!' cried Hiccup,
triumphantly. 'I have trained your untrainable dragon to
be more obedient than your own hunting-dragons! You
gave us the Word of a Chief that you would forget the
insult to your Tribe, and so we can keep our Hooligan
heads on our Hooligan shoulders!'

HA HA HA HA HA HA HA! roared the crowd.

'It does look like the Hooligan boy is right,' smiled
UG the Uglithug.

'At least he's trained that Hogfly of yours to fetch.'
Mogadon the Meathead smiled. 'But I'm quite surprised
that your other hunting-dragons are so disobedient,
Very-Vicious. Maybe you Visithugs aren't yelling loud
enough. . . Perhaps you've gone *soft,*' he jeered.

Very-Vicious the Visithug had a dim idea that he
had been tricked in some way.

But the Word of a Chief has to be kept.

Very-Vicious stomped forward. He gathered up the
Hogfly and tickled him on the tummy, making a fuss of
him.

'You win, weirdo-boy,' growled Very-Vicious.

'Nobody dies today. And you can keep my other hunting-dragons, the ones that did not obey. The Very-Vicious Tribe has no use for disobedient dragons.'

And then Very-Vicious climbed aboard his riding-dragon and took off for the Visithug Territories, signalling to his Tribe to follow, the blissfully happy little Hogfly cradled in his great hairy arms.

'Bye-bye, Hogfly. . .' whispered Hiccup, waving to the little Hogfly, who barked back, 'Thank you, Grandma!'

'We'll miss you. . .'

'N-n-no, we won't!' said Toothless, climbing on top of Hiccup's helmet and giving a victory *cock-a-doodle-doo.*

Once the Visithug Tribe was at a safe distance, Stoick the Vast swelled in triumph, and shook his fist at their departing dragons. 'OFF YOU GO, YOU VISITHUG COWARDS!' he bellowed happily. 'DON'T YOU KNOW NOT TO MESS WITH US HOOLIGANS?'

HA HA HA HA HA HA HA! roared the appreciative crowd.

'Well, I think that went rather well, don't you, Hiccup?' Stoick rubbed his hands together briskly. 'You showed everyone what wonderful dragon trainers the Hooligan Tribe are. . . And we've gained rather a lot of magnificent hunting-dragons into the bargain. It couldn't be bet— *Oh!*'

Stoick gave an anxious start as a huge, hairy hand tapped him on the shoulder. 'Dastardly Dangerus! I'd forgotten about *you!*'

Hiccup hadn't forgotten.

Poor Toothless gave an unhappy whine, and hid in Hiccup's backpack again. He'd hoped that the dreadful little red-haired girl might have forgotten about him.

'It's always unwise to forget about us Danger-Brutes,' said Dastardly Dangerus with a smile. 'My Hullaballoo beat all your Young Warriors in the Dragon Sprint, so your Hooligan Tribes have lost against us, Stoick the Vast. Therefore you owe me a hunting-dragon.'

'And I want that one!' shrieked Nettle. 'Thweetie ith hiding in the skinny boyth backpack!'

Dastardly stretched out a huge hand and lifted up Hiccup's backpack.

And there was poor Toothless.

'B-b-but Toothless is H-h-hiccup's dragon,' wept poor Toothless, miserably, flying up into Hiccup's arms.

Stoick swallowed.

'Well now, Dastardly, I happen to have acquired several extremely valuable and rare Visithug hunting-dragons,' he said. 'How about having those instead of the toothless dragon? My son, you see, is kind of fond of this strange little creature, Thor only knows why. . .'

'I want **THAT ONE!**' squealed Nettle, holding out her arms towards poor Toothless in excitement.

Stoick sighed. 'I'm sorry, son,' he said, heavily. 'You're going to have to hand over *Goofless*. A Hooligan's word is sacred. . . I have given my Word as a Chief, and the Word of a Chief must be kept. . .'

Hiccup's mind raced.

'Hang on just *one second. . .*' he said.

He ran to the bonfire that had been lit in honour of the Games.

He took the Throatgoggler egg and thrust it into the fire.

'HICCUP!' roared Stoick. 'A HOOLIGAN ALWAYS HONOURS HIS BETS!'

Toothless was now passionately clasped around Hiccup's neck. 'D-d-don't send me away, Master...'

'One second...' whispered Hiccup. 'Just one second...'
The egg inside the bonfire began to shake... It

turned white, then purple. . . and, just as a flash of white-hot lightning shot out of the fire (and MOST unfortunately hit Snotlout, burning off both his eyebrows) the egg exploded into little green fragments. . .

. . . and a tiny little Throatgoggler dragon, about two inches high, staggered out of the fire. . .

Hiccup took out his helmet and carefully caught the tiny little dragon, for it was still SMOKING hot.

Toothless gave a snort of revulsion.

Dastardly Dangerus and Stoick paused, blinking through the clouds of mustardy-green gas that had been released by the exploding egg. . .

Nettle had her mouth open to scream for Toothless again, but she took a good, hard look at the little Throatgoggler dragon Hiccup was holding out towards her.

It's a curious thing about dragon babies.

Sometimes the most terrifying, the most deadly, the most *ruthless* of dragon species, have the cutest little babies.

The Throatgoggler baby is particularly adorable.

It is so small it can fit snugly into a teaspoon.

It has dear little goggly eyes.

Its scales are so soft it is practically fluffy.

It makes precious little goggling noises in its ickle, tiny throat.

Nettle took one look at that dear little Throatgoggler dragon peering up at her over the rim of Hiccup's helmet, and she whispered: 'I changed my mind. I want *that* dragon, Daddy.'

Dastardly Dangerus swallowed. He had a dim

goggle...

The Throatgoggle.
dragon is particularly
adorable.

feeling that this particular dragon might not be such a good idea.

'Are you sure about that, my little precious?'

A stern note came into Nettle's voice. 'I WANT THAT DRAGON, DADDY...'

'OK, my sweetness,' said Dastardly Dangerus, hurriedly. 'Hand over the frog-like dragon, then, Stoick's Odd-Looking Son.'

Hiccup handed the dragon over to Nettle.

Nettle looked down at the little creature with love. 'I thall call her Thweetie,' said Nettle, firmly. 'And I want to take her HOME.'

'Well, you can take her home AFTER the banquet, snookums,' coaxed Dastardly Dangerus.

'I wanth to go home NOW,' said Nettle. 'Ith my bedtime...'

The Danger-Brutes left after that, to Stoick's immense relief. He'd had quite enough of them, what with one thing and another: he hadn't got over them destroying his Chiefly Hut, and he didn't want them spoiling the Banquet at the end of the Games.

And as the last Danger-Brute dragon disappeared over the horizon, Stoick felt they were sufficiently far away to shout:

317

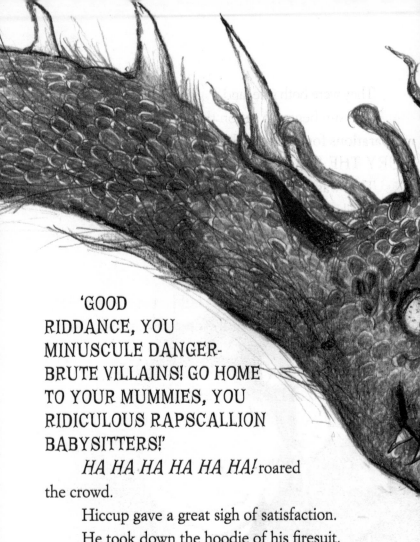

'GOOD
RIDDANCE, YOU
MINUSCULE DANGER-
BRUTE VILLAINS! GO HOME
TO YOUR MUMMIES, YOU
RIDICULOUS RAPSCALLION
BABYSITTERS!'

HA HA HA HA HA HA! roared
the crowd.

Hiccup gave a great sigh of satisfaction.
He took down the hoodie of his firesuit.
He put on his helmet.
The Quest was completed.
Windwalker licked his face.
Toothless snuggled up to him.

318

They were both safe, and that was the important thing.

The sun began to set on the horizon, and the preparations for the Inter-Tribe Summer-tide Friendly BURY THE HACHET Games Banquet began.

That was a happy, bustly, joyful nightfall, with all of the Tribes working together, setting up tables on the Long Beach and telling jokes, and building fires

and cooking delicious stews as the moon rose and they prepared for a long night of celebration.

'You see, Hiccup?' roared Stoick, several hours later, happily munching on a huge portion of fish, as he sat with all the Tribes around a massive bonfire. The brilliant canopy of stars in the night sky above was reflected in the glass-flat sea below, waves gently breaking on the sand. 'My BURY THE HACHET Games was a good idea after all!'

Stoick beamed with satisfaction. 'All of the Tribes working together. . . Even UG the Uglithug is here and no Blood Feuds broke out. . . Everything turned out all right in the end.'

Hiccup looked around at the Vikings of the Archipelago, patting each other on the back and raising toasts and singing songs, and he had to admit that it was a wonderful moment of harmony.

'Plus, I got myself some of the very latest hunting-dragons, and the Hooligans kept their reputation as brilliant dragon trainers!' boomed Stoick. 'Leave the politics to me, Hiccup, leave the politics to me. . .'

Camicazi had already finished her meal and was doing a jig on one of the tables. She was juggling three of Chief Dastardly Dangerus's favourite knives, and Chief

Very-Vicious's lucky gold shark tooth, which she had cleverly pick-pocketed during the recent commotion. She then began doing an impression of Chief Dastardly Dangerus being ordered about by Nettle, which had everybody in stitches.

Fishlegs was staring in an awed sort of way at UG the Uglithug's daughter, Tantrum, who was about six foot two with a lot of flame-red hair and green eyes.

'Wow. . .' whispered Fishlegs, blushing furiously. 'What a beautiful princess. . .'

The beautiful princess sulkily picked her nose with the tip of her axe. (This is not to be recommended, by the way. Picking your nose with your axe is DANGEROUS.)

WoW, What a beautiful princess..

'I think I should write that beautiful princess a poem. . .' whispered Fishlegs. 'If I'm going to be a bard, I really need a MUSE. . .'

Now MOST unfortunately Hiccup wasn't concentrating on Fishlegs at that moment, because if he had heard Fishlegs saying this he could have pointed out that sending love-poems to the only daughters of chiefs who are homicidal maniacs really is a gobsmackingly bad idea.

And if you are a keen and sharp-eyed reader of these adventures, you will realise that this would have changed the whole course of history.

If Hiccup had been concentrating at that moment, Fishlegs would never have written that love-poem, and Hiccup would never have gone to the little isle of Berserk, the Dragon Furious would never have been released, the dragons would never have declared war on the humans. . .

And so on.

A whole chain of catastrophic events would have been avoided if only Hiccup had been concentrating at that moment.

But, unfortunately, the world turns on tiny, seemingly insignificant events such as these.

Fishlegs' words were soft, the hubbub of general merriment was loud, and Hiccup wasn't really listening. And why wasn't he listening?

Toothless had spotted something in the night-time sky, and he had flown down to warn Hiccup: 'Throatgogglers! Them Throatgogglers is coming to get b-b-back their egg!'

Hiccup had been staring up at the sky, his dagger drawn, trying to alert his father as he scanned the night: 'Yes, but as I keep saying, Father. . . it's *not* quite the end. I've been trying to tell you about these Throatgoggler dragons, and I'm worried they might be going to attack us, thinking we still have something that belongs to them—'

'You worry too much, Hiccup!' roared Stoick.

'And there they are. . .' whispered Hiccup, tensing, as way, way up in the airy heights, clustering in front of the moon like a mass of distant black flies, he could see the shapes of thousands and thousands of Throatgogglers.

For a moment they hung there.

Hiccup held his breath, his dagger poised. . .

323

And then the mass of Throatgogglers flew to the west, heading for Danger-Brute territory, after Dastardly-Dangerus and the baby Throatgoggler.

'You're right, Camicazi,' said Hiccup thoughtfully. 'Dragons should be free to come and go, like Stormfly here.'

Hiccup had been wondering about this for a while, but this entire incident had really confirmed his worries.

'Too right they should,' sniffed Camicazi approvingly, who had wandered over to sit next to Hiccup. 'Those Throatgogglers are going to give the Danger-Brutes a very hard time when they get to the Danger-Brute islands...'

The Danger-Brutes did indeed have a very rough night fighting off those Throatgogglers. And in the course of the battle, in order to get the Throatgogglers to leave them alone, Dastardly Dangerus had to release every single prisoner, both human and dragon, being held in the ghastly Dungeons of the Danger-Brutes. And Nettle lost the baby Throatgoggler dragon, which flew off with its mother when she came to rescue it, back to their home in the Gorge of the Thunderbolt of Thor.

Nobody seemed very sad about this.

'Sweetie!' huffed Toothless, still outraged. 'The little human wanted to call me Sweetie! Me! The terror of the Inner Isles, to be called Sweetie!'

Both Stormfly and Windwalker shook their heads at the generally shocking behaviour of humans towards dragons.

Down on Long Beach, Hiccup was very relieved to see the Throatgogglers pass Berk by, and he sheathed his dagger.

'Wow. . .' he said. 'Throatgogglers really are the most brilliant tracker-dragons. They must have sensed that the baby Throatgoggler had been taken off by the Danger-Brutes. I must put that in my *Guide to Dragons and their Eggs*. . .'

'What are you talking about?' bellowed Stoick, mouth full of food and delightfully unaware that, at that very moment, he could have been having a full-on battle with one of the most dangerous species of dragons you could find in the Archipelago.

'Nothing!' Hiccup grinned, picking up a forkful of stew. 'Now I can relax. What were you saying, Fishlegs?'

'Nothing,' mumbled Fishlegs, blushing to the roots of his helmet.

A pause.

Hiccup, Fishlegs and Camicazi sat next to each other on the sand, in comfortable, happy silence, eating up their suppers, with the joyful sound of singing, and the merry noise of Vikings toasting each other in the background.

Hiccup put down his fork. He had a friend on either side of him, and Stormfly was snuggled on Camicazi's lap, occasionally reaching out and stealing the best bits from Hiccup's plate.

The adventure was over, his father hadn't lost his head, and he hadn't lost Toothless, so he should have been perfectly content – but something was still bothering him.

He remembered what it was, and reached into his bag that had the training apples in it.

'What have you got there, Hiccup?' asked Camicazi, sitting beside Hiccup on the sand.

Hiccup was staring at the object in his hand. 'Oh, the Hogfly had it in his mouth when he dropped the egg. I think he must have found it in the gorge. . . or. . . I'm not quite sure where it came from, actually. It was sticking to the egg, all tangled up in seaweed. . . How strange!'

The something, now Hiccup was able to look at it closely, was a single chess piece: a king.

There was a small brown stain on the head, as if it might have been blood.

A little shiver ran down his spine as Hiccup looked at it, as if he knew this chess piece was going to be significant in his life in the future. . .

I'll think about this tomorrow, thought Hiccup, and he put the chess piece back in his pocket.

'Now THIS,' he said, his mouth full of stew, 'really *is* a happy ending. My father is right. I worry too much.'

THE END

EPILOGUE BY HICCUP HORRENDOUS HADDOCK THE THIRD, THE LAST OF THE GREAT VIKING HEROES

These adventures both took place a long, long time ago, back when I was a boy.

Little did I know it then, but that first adventure with the Green Death, when I found Toothless in a cave on Death's Head Headland, was also the first step in my Quest to find the King's Lost Things, so that I could become the King of the Wilderwest and save the dragons from extinction.

Toothless, the fang-free dragon, was the first Lost Thing. But there were nine more Lost Things, and I would have to collect them all if I wanted to save the dragons.

It may be that when you are reading this book in the future, you are wondering why you don't see so many dragons round about you.

What happened to them? Did I save them?

You will have to read my twelve *How To Train Your Dragon* adventures to find out if I found the Lost Things and succeeded in that Quest.

So, it was not THE END at all.

You see, this is the thing about stories.

Just when you think things are THE END, sometimes they have the fragments of something that might turn into a new beginning.

A little itch. A little detail. Something small and surprising that arrived by accident and then grows into something much larger and more important than you thought it was at the time.

Just as Fishlegs' poem to Tantrum was going to set off a whole load of unfortunate and unforeseen consequences. . .

. . . so, too, was I right, all those years ago, back at the feast on Long Beach. That chess piece wasn't one of the King's Lost Things, but it was still going to be Very Significant Indeed, a long, long time into my future, even after the Great Dragon Rebellion ended in the twelfth book of my memoirs.

However, my father Stoick was right, too.

Even though the beginnings of new adventures, new heartaches, had already begun, and trouble was just around the corner, lurking on the horizon, even though UG and his Uglithugs had already dug up their hatchets, on the pretext of using them to bash open their crab claws. . .

I can still hear in my head the joyful songs ringing out from my fellow Vikings all around me as we sat under the starry, starry sky that long ago night on the little isle of Berk.

'THE HERO CARES NOT FOR A WILD WINTER'S STORM,
FOR IT CARRIES HIM SWIFT ON THE BACK OF A WAVE,
ALL MAY BE LOST AND OUR HEARTS MAY BE WORN
BUT A HERO... FIGHTS... FOREVER!'

And I can still see the smoke curling out from the nose of the sleeping Windwalker, and feel Toothless in my waistcoat, snoring away, pressing against my chest. That was the moment when I realised that dragons really ought to be free, and in the wilderness where they belonged, even though my heart ached at the unbearable thought of ever losing Toothless, of a world without Windwalker.

Hurt me as it may, the dragons needed to feel as free as the winds under their wings. . .

. . . and *I* needed to fight for that.

It was going to be difficult, I thought to myself, looking around at my fellow Vikings. Even Camicazi, whose dragon Stormfly came and went as she pleased, why, even *she* didn't yet believe in freeing the dragons *entirely*. Furthermore, everyone already felt I was a bit of a mistake – an accident, a 'hiccup' if you like – as a member of the Hooligan Tribe, so if I started talking about letting the dragons go back into the wild, they would imagine I had lost the plot entirely. Maybe it was a lost cause... Perhaps it was an Impossible Quest. . . Why did I think that fighting this hopeless crusade was going to be *my* responsibility? I asked myself crossly. Why me? Why not someone else?

Because, and I answered my own question, all those long years ago. . .

However treacherous the path may be through the heather, however difficult it is for you to say what needs to be said, however small and helpless and unimportant you might look, you always have to fight with your heart and your hands and your head, for what you believe to be right.

For when the world needs a Hero. . .

. . . it might as well be YOU.

Toothless snorted in his sleep, jolting me out of my thoughts, and I shook off my introspective mood.

Not yet, though, I thought. *I don't have to be that big Hero* YET.

And I am happy to remember that I joined my fellow Vikings in singing the last verse of the 'Hero' song as if I hadn't a care in the world.

For this is all we have, this beautiful, flawed, boggy green island in a blue sea, and this imperfect minute that we are so blessed to be living in.

And we have to enjoy it and embrace it and sing our thanks when we can.

'YOU ARE NEVER ALONE IF THE SEA IS
YOUR FRIEND,
RIDING THE WAVES OF IMPOSSIBLE
QUESTS,
IF IT DOESN'T END WELL, THEN IT ISN'T
THE END,
FOR A HERO... IS... FOREVER!'

A Hero is forever.

Here is a packet that was found by a team of archeologists searching in caves nearby to the beach where the original memoirs were discovered , including this 'lost' story about the Hogfly. It was hidden underneath a rock, and the items within were perfectly preserved. Hiccup's birth certificate is particularly interesting for historians, for it provides a reason why he was given the name of 'Hiccup'.

Although the packet looks like it is made out of the skin of a crocodile or lizard, in fact the DNA shows it to be that of some unique species never before seen by man.

Birth  Certificate

Child's name given by the Archipelago Naming Dame:

Hiccup Horrendous Haddock the Third (RUNT)

Reasons for given name:

I examined the child and found him to be sickly and undersized and therefore pronounced him a RUNT, and gave him the name of HICCUP, the traditional name for a RUNT in the Hooligan Tribe. I advised that he should be exposed on the mountainside or set to sea alone in a small boat in order that Fate and the gods should deal with him. In this way the strength of the Hooligan Tribe will not be weakened.

Unfortunately his father, Stoick the Vast would not allow the boy to be killed, in strict defiance of our Laws.

Name of Father:

STOICK HORRENDOUS HADDOCK, known as 'the Vast', Chief of the Hairy Hooligan Tribe

Name of Mother:

Valhallarama of the White Arms **OVER MY DEAD BODY**

Place of Birth:

Isle of Berk, Barbaric Archipelago

Date of Birth:

29th February of a Leap Year, Dark Ages.
(Another sign that the child is a RUNT)

Signature of Naming Dame:

Hagiella de Meany

THIS CERTIFICAT MUST BE DESTROYED. STOICK THE VAST.

Toss out the freak or the Tribe shall be weak

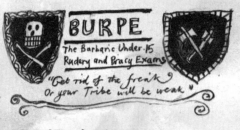

BURPE
The Barbaric Under-15
Rudery and Bracy Exams
"Get rid of the freak
Or your Tribe will be weak"

"Toss out the weird,
And your Tribe will be feared"

Name of candidate:

Fishlegs ... No-Name-
Because: Abandoned in
a lobster pot as a baiting

LEVEL ONE: One hour

Smoking and spitting is permitted during the exammination.
Extra marks will be givven four badd speling and pore handwriting.

Begin at sound of fogghorn.

Question 1: Give a short explanation for the decline of the Roman Empire (2 marks)

I hadn't realised they were declining ✓✓ ½. They have wonderful
art. XXX! 0 marks for second bit, but nise
iggnorance at the beggining

Question 2: How do you trane a dragon? (4 marks)

Beg. XXX READ YORE YOBBISH
0 marks.

Question 3: A Gaulish fishing boat is blown off course into Archipelago waters. How do you act? (2 marks)

Ask them if you can get a lift back to Gaul.
XX SEE ME
0 marks

Question 4: You suspect that the Visithugs may have been stealing your sheep. The political situation is delicate. What do you do? (2 marks)

Nothing at all. These Visithugs are TOUGH. X 0 marks

Question 5: Find X:
(2 marks)

5cm

X — Here is the
X ✓ 1 mark

4cm

Marks out of 10

2

Examiners comments: Well tried, but pitifully
pore. GOBBER the BELCH

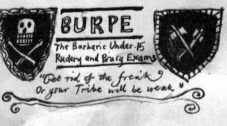

BURPE
The Barbaric Under-15 Rudery and Bracy Exams
"Get rid of the freak
Or your Tribe will be weak"

"Toss out the weird,
And your Tribe will be feared"

Name of candidate:

Hiccup Horrendous
Haddock the Third
Heir to the Chief
of the Hooligan Tribe

LEVEL ONE: One hour

Smoking and spitting <u>is</u> permitted during the exammination.
Extra marks will be givven four badd speling and pore handwriting.

Begin at sound of fogghorn.

Question 1: Give a short explanation for the decline of the Roman Empire (2 marks)

Well, this is a very interessing question. The Roman economy has been disintegrating for some time now, and although the Eastern Roman Empire is still going strong

XO marks
P.T.O

Question 2: How do you trane a dragon? (4 marks)

Another interesting question. I find COMMUNICATION is very important P.TO.

← WOT??? X 0 marks

Question 3: A Gaulish fishing boat is blown off course into Archipelago waters. How do you act? (2 marks)

I would say "Excusez-moi, mon brave, mais c'est very partin? La France est par là..." X 0 marks SEE ME

Question 4: You suspect that the Visithugs may have been stealing your sheep. The political situation is delicate. What do you do? (2 marks)

VERY LONG WORDS, HICCUP

Well, first I would send out diplomatic envoys to check that it really was them, and then I would
P.T.O

Question 5: Find X: (2 marks)

5cm

X

4cm

X = 3
X NO! VIKINGS DON'T DO MATHS

Marks out of 10

◯

Examiners comments: Very disapointing, Hiccup, I think you are strugging with the basicks of beinn a Viking. SEE ME. Gobber the Belch

BURPE
The Barbaric Under-15 Rudery and Bracy Exams

"Get rid of the freak
Or your Tribe will be weak"

"Toss out the weird,
And your Tribe will be feared"

Name of candidate:
Snotface Snotlout
3rd in line to be
Chief of the
HOOLIGAN Tribe and
won't I make a good

LEVEL ONE: One hour

Smoking and spitting is permitted during the examination.
Extra marks will be givven four badd speling and pore handwriting.

Begin at sound of fog horn.

Question 1: Give a short explanation for the decline of the Roman Empire (2 marks)

Who cares??? Those Rommans got too fat to fight. ✓ 2 marks
Good answer

Question 2: How do you trane a dragon? (4 marks)

YELL 'AT IT. ✓ 4 marks
Well done boy. Yoo read yor yobbish.

Question 3: A Gaulish fishing boat is blown off course into Archipelago waters. How do you act? (2 marks)

I wood steel everything inkluding there trowsers. ✓✓ 2 marks

Question 4: You suspect that the Visithugs may have been stealing your sheep. The political situation is delicate. What do you do? (2 marks)

Start a blud Feud. Those Visithugs are mackerel braned burglars. ✓✓✓

Question 5: Find X: (2 marks)

5cm
X
4cm

I neither know nor care. ✓✓ 2 marks

Marks out of 10

13

Examiners comments: Luvly work Snotlout. Yoo are a pleshure to teach. GOBBER THE BELCH

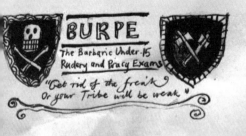

BURPE
The Barbaric Under-15
Rudery and Brucy Exams

"Get rid of the freak
Or your Tribe will be weak"

"Toss out the weird,
And your Tribe will be feared"

Name of candidate:

Dogsbreth the Durbrane ✓/1 mark

Smoking and spitting <u>is</u> permitted during the exammination.
Extra marks will be givven four badd speling and pore handwriting.

Begin at sound of fogghorn.

Question 1: Give a short explanation for the decline of the Roman Empire (2 marks)

WOT? ✓✓ Eggsdent 2 marks Iggnorance

Question 2: How do you trane a dragon? (4 marks)

Eat it. Ha Ha Ha ✗ ½ marks

Question 3: A Gaulish fishing boat is blown off course into Archipelago waters. How do you act? (2 marks)

I wood say wot R yoo looking at, sunshine? and then I wood thump them. ✓✓ 2

Question 4: You suspect that the Visithugs may have been stealing your sheep. The political situation is delicate. What do you do? (2 marks)

Moore thumping. ✓ 2
stop asking mee QWESTHUNS!!

Find X:
(2 marks)

5cm
X
4cm

Examiners comments: Yoo are a natyrally GIFFTED Barbarrian. Wett dun. Gobber the Belch

Could this be the proof
that dragons really existed?

This is a drawing of the **Dragon Jewel**, *a very rare and impossibly valuable amulet traditionally worn by the Kings of the Wilderwest when they were crowned.*

The Dragon Jewel consists of a piece of amber about the size of a pigeon's egg, inside which there are two exquisite little nanodragons, with a tail in each other's mouth. They must have been fighting when they were caught in the molten amber, centuries before, and the amber then solidified, so the dragons are preserved forever in the fiery golden substance, in perpetual suspended animation.

The Dragon Jewel is the Holy Grail of paleontology for if it were ever to be discovered, it would finally prove the existence of dragons.

This drawing is being held under armed guard at a secret location while it is studied by scientists for clues as to the Jewel's whereabouts. It is rumoured that Hiccup himself wrote on the back of the drawing. The exact words have not yet been released to the public yet.

Learning to Speak Dragonese

Dragonese can be rather embarrassing to speak because there are lots of odd sounds and accents like whistling, clicking and strange low farting noises.

Here are some common phrases:

Pishyou na flicka-flame bum-support.
Please do not set fire to the chair.

Grab-claw di stink-fish or me do di heebi-jeebys.
Just hunt me a haddock, or I'm really going to lose it.

Hoody wobble-di-gats in di bath-juice de mamma?
Who has been sick in my mother's bath-water?

Bathtime

When a dragon has spent the whole day in a mud wallow and they then want to curl up in your bed you have no option. YOU HAVE TO GIVE THEM A BATH. Good luck.

Dragon: Me na wash di bum. Me na wash di face. Me na wash di claws. Me na splishy oo di splashy ATALL.
I do not want a bath.

You are going to have to be cunning and use PSYCHOLOGY.

You: Na bathtime ever never ever never. Me repeeti. Na bathtime EVER NEVER. On no account are you to get in the bath.

Dragon (whining): Me wanti splishy splashy.
You: Okey dokey just wun time.
All right just this once.

Hoody drunken di bath juice?
Who has drunk up the bath water?

toilet training

The time has come to toilet train your dragon. You are going to have to be very patient about this. Here are some phrases you might find useful:

You: Toothless, ta COGLET me wantee ta cack-cack in di greenclaw cackspot...
Toothless, you KNOW I want you to poo in the dragon toilets...

Dragon: O yessee yessee, me coglet...
Yes, yes, I know...

You: (pointing at large poo in the middle of Stoick's bed) Erg... questa SA?
So what, then, is THIS?

PAUSE

Dragon (hopefully): Ummm... un chocklush snik-snak?
Er... a chocolate biscuit?

You: Snotta chocklush snik-snak, issa CACK-CACK, issa cack-cack di Toothless NA in di greenclaw cackspot, may oopla bang splosh in di middling di sleepy-slab di pappa.
This isn't a chocolate biscuit, it's a POO, it's one of YOUR poos, Toothless, and it ISN'T in the dragon toilets, it's right bang splat in the middle of my father's bed.

You don't **HAVE** to read the
HOW TO TRAIN YOUR DRAGON books in order.
But if you want to, this is the right order:

1. How to train your Dragon
2. How to be a Pirate
3. How to speak Dragonese
4. How to Cheat a Dragon's Curse
5. How to Twist a Dragon's Tale
6. A Hero's Guide to Deadly Dragons
7. How to Ride a Dragon's Storm
8. How to Break a Dragon's Heart
9. How to Steal a Dragon's Sword
10. How to Seize a Dragon's Jewel
11. How to Betray a Dragon's Hero
12. How to Fight a Dragon's Fury